of the
FRIENDS
OF
Washoe County Library

BETH KEPHART

The Heart *Is Not a* Size

HARPER TEEN
An Imprint of HarperCollins*Publishers*

The poem discussed on page 65, "Laundry," is an original poem by Beth Kephart. The article quoted on page 93, "The World Hands Project: Anapra, Mexico" by J. Matthew Thomas, is from *Forward*, a journal of the National Associates Committee of the American Institute of Architects, Fall 2008. http://info.aia.org/nwsltr_nacq.cfm?pagename=nacq_a_060112_special_topic_thomas. The lines on page 112 and 184 are from "Tear It Down" by Jack Gilbert, which appeared in *The Great Fires: Poems, 1982–1992* by Jack Gilbert, published by Alfred A. Knopf, 1994. The lines on page 196 are from "A Brief for the Defense" by Jack Gilbert, which appeared in *Refusing Heaven: Poems* by Jack Gilbert, published by Alfred A. Knopf, 2005.

HarperTeen is an imprint of HarperCollins Publishers.

The Heart Is Not a Size
 For information address HarperCollins Children's Books, a division of HarperCollins Publishers, 10 East 53rd Street, New York, NY 10022.
www.harperteen.com

Library of Congress Cataloging-in-Publication Data

Kephart, Beth.

The heart is not a size / Beth Kephart. — 1st ed.

p. cm. — (Harperteen)

Summary: Fifteen-year-old Georgia learns a great deal about herself and her troubled best friend, Riley, when they become part of a group of suburban Pennsylvania teenagers who go to Anapra, a squatters' village in the border town of Juárez, Mexico, to undertake a community construction project.

ISBN 978-0-06-147048-6 (trade bdg.)

[1. Self-perception—Fiction. 2. Best friends—Fiction. 3. Friendship—Fiction. 4. Voluntarism—Fiction. 5. Poverty—Fiction. 6. Conduct of life—Fiction. 7. Ciudad Juárez (Mexico)—Fiction. 8. Mexico—Fiction.] I. Title.

PZ7.K438He 2010 2008055721
[Fic]—dc22 CIP
AC

Typography by Carla Weise

10 11 12 13 14 15 CG/RRDB 10 9 8 7 6 5 4 3 2 1

❖

First Edition

For Jeremy,

who lived Juárez with me,

and whose own heart knows no measure

Prologue

What I remember now is the bunch of them running: from the tins, which were their houses. Up the white streets, which were the color of bone. All the way to the top of Anapra, to where we were standing in our secondhand scrubs and where Riley said, "They might as well be flowers, blown right off their stalks," and Sophie said, "This is so completely *wild*," and the Third said nothing at all. The Third: He wasn't talking yet. He was all size and silence.

"I should tell Mack," I said, but I didn't budge, didn't even turn and glance back toward where Mack and the others were digging in, hanging tarp, toting two-by-fours from one angle of sun fizzle to another. Because the kids of Anapra might have been chunks of blown-off petals, like Riley said, but they mostly looked like wings to me, flying and flying in their bright, defiant best; their yellow cotton shirts, red fringy skirts, blue trousers. They looked like something no one should lose to a single instant of forgetting.

It was only our second day.

We'd pinned everything on nothing.

We'd flown south through the swill of a storm, ready for service. On the runway the rain against the plane had been the sound of slash, and then there was the high kick of altitude, and then the stitch of lightning through the chunking gray-green clouds. Finally we were through all that and into nothing but blue, the clouds a horrifying plunge below. I was window-seated beside a kid named Corey, who was friends with Sam and Jazzy but not with me; I was thinking about how, up so high, there was nothing to measure distance with. The sky was blue, just that one color—blue. You could fly forever and never get one inch closer to the sun.

Riley was back in seat 15B, accessorized with her hot-pink iPod, her twenty-two beaded bracelets. She'd snatched the tortoiseshell claw from the back of her head before we'd boarded, letting her yellow-streaked-with-orange hair go messy around her shoulders, and she was swamped by this olive T-shirt with these fuchsia letters that would have won any prize, she boasted, for ugly. Riley had one of those freckle mists over the bridge of her nose and eyes the guys called sapphire. She had thirteen hoops that hung like minitambourine jingles from her left ear. She was smarter than she'd let most people believe; but she was private about that, just as she was with most things. Going to Anapra was the pact we'd made. *If you go, I'll go:* That was our mantra.

Of course, Riley's parents thought that I'd be looking out for her, that I'd make sure that nothing lousy happened. That's the problem with the way I am—big boned, brown haired, straight-backed, steady, and therefore (anyone can do the calculation) revoltingly responsible. When you're seventeen years old and you've never kissed a boy and you're in all the honors classes, when you can't stand the thought of sticking fingers into your eyes so you still wear glasses and not contact lenses, when you're the middle child of three, you have what comes down to no choice. All the neighbors choose you for their cat sitting. All the summer camps want you as their aide. All the parents suggest to their kids: *You should be friends with Georgia.* I was what passed for safe in a hapless world.

Or, at least, to most people I was.

PART *One*

one

It was a sign thumbtacked high on the corkboard of the local Acme. A flyer, really—quick-copy-shop mauve and nothing fancy. The headline read TWO WEEKS THAT WILL CHANGE YOUR LIFE—another famous preposterous promise, and so I stopped to read it. I find it humorous, what claims get made in the interest of stirring up business. I find it relaxing, reading the things they stick to the cork at the local grocery store.

So it wasn't the headline that suckered me in; it was the smaller-type info. The stuff about traveling south of the border, to the great Mexican nation. The promises about building community. *Participants will come together for a shared purpose,* the flyer said. *They'll live and work with the people of Juárez on behalf of those with nothing.* Twelve people my age were being solicited for the summer trip, plus two adult chaperones. If you wanted to know more, you could ring up GoodWorks or visit the web. I read the thing through twice, and after that all the other nearby flyers and tabs and desperate pleas for house sitters and dog sitters and nannies. Then I called Riley.

"Hey," I said.

"What's up?" It was Christmas break of our junior year, four days past the presents. She was downloading songs to her iPod.

"I'm at the Acme," I told her.

Riley groaned. "Reading the corkboard again?"

"Precisely," I said. "Reading the corkboard."

"Don't you have a Lit thing due?"

"I do. But this is better."

"And?"

"And I've made a discovery."

"Can't wait." She big-yawned. "What's that?"

"You ever heard of Juárez?"

"That's a battleship, right? Or, like, the name of a painter?"

"Wrong again."

"What do you expect?"

"Your best every time, Riley. Always."

"Okay, so what's Juárez?" she said, after she remembered I was still waiting.

"A place," I said. "In Mexico. Do you mind if I come over?"

From the Acme to Riley's took thirty minutes walking. By bike I could get there in ten. There was a small stretch of ugliness before you got to the perfect prettiness of Riley's neighborhood, where every mini-mansion sat on a hill and was connected to the street by a cobbled drive. They'd chewed up a farm to make room for the homes, and then they'd gone and rooted in new trees—little spindles that gave off no shade and hardly dirtied the emerald-colored lawns with fallen leaves. In the winter those trees looked like shiver, all lit with Christmas doodads.

At Riley's, which was the biggest house on the tallest hill, there must have been two dozen of those minuscule birches—twelve on one side of the cobbled drive, twelve on the other—all of them done up with blinking reds, greens, whites. I had to walk my bike to the top of that hill. I parked it around back and out of sight—rule number 37,854 of Riley's more-perfect-than-most-perfect mother. I called Riley after I parked. She let me in through the back door and I went up the set of back stairs. It was easier than going the front-door route and drinking ginger tea with Riley's mom.

Riley was sprawled out as usual when I found her, looking tinier than ever in her pink-frilled, queen-sized bed. She had a bunch of pillows at her head and the buds of her iPod plugged in. She was doing a squiggle dance on her back like a flipped-over turtle, but when she saw me she yanked at her ear buds, slapped the edge of the mattress, and invited me to sit down.

"Do you have an encyclopedia in this room?" I asked, looking past her now to the wall of shelves where she kept every scrap of collected thing. Used water bottles, lacrosse medals, *People* magazines, the little dolls that her parents used to bring her from their around-the-world trips—*excursions*, they called them. There were sketches she'd never developed for art and sculptures that had gone screwy and buckled watercolor portraits; there was a bunch of books lying sideways, like props—little stages on which sat the fuzzy elephants and neon monkeys from the Devon Horse Show, where we'd gone every year since we were kids and where Riley inevitably won at the water pistol booth.

"Maybe," Riley said. "Somewhere. Why?"

"Juárez?" I said. "Remember?"

I tilted my head sideways to read the names of the books, pushed my glasses up on the bridge of my nose. Finally I found something that said *World Atlas*. Probably some gift from some aunt somewhere. Clearly not a book Riley'd ever opened. "You mind?" I asked, starting to shift things around—moving a stuffed turkey to the ledge of another book, shifting a squeaky mouse to a shelf below. When Riley didn't answer, I turned around. She had her ear buds back in. She was dancing.

Flipping through the pages of the atlas, I got to Mexico in no time, then found Juárez, which is directly across the Rio Grande from the Texas town of El Paso. Fourth largest city in Mexico, the atlas said. Home of the final battle of the Mexican Revolution. Sited along the famous El Camino Real. Juárez is a border town, a real place, in an atlas. Google makes a lot of promises, I've found. An atlas goes sturdy with the facts.

"Riley," I said. "Please." I pantomimed about the ear buds until she plucked them out.

"What's up?"

"We're going to Juárez," I said.

She laughed her lovely Riley laugh. I sat beside her, let her laugh.

two

All I had to do to convince my mom to give me two weeks off was to promise her a rest-of-summer's worth of babysitting. My younger brother, Kev, was nine going on 150 miles per hour. He was all Fantastic Four wrapped into one; and his most death-defying mission was messing with Geoff, my older, bound-for-college brother. My mother volunteered mornings at the local library. Every summer, she begged me to make sure Kev stayed alive. "Just don't let him hurt himself" was her favorite line, and then she'd close the door and go to her morning of superlatively well-behaved library books, to rooms that were so quiet you could hear a pencil snap. I offered my mother a—she loved the word—reprieve. I was the someone Kev mostly obeyed. Geoff had no patience, never had, not for his little brother. I said that if she let me go off to Juárez, I'd be home afterward, available every library morning from mid-July through the day that school began.

"Do you know anything about Juárez?" she asked me. "Anything at all?" She was cleaning out the refrigerator, ditching what she called her science experiments. A startling blue-green mold had started to web across a tomato. "Well, that's pretty," she said, and tossed it. She crouched again and fished out a bag of half-used mozzarella and a block of white-pocked cheddar. "I'm not buying cheese for another year," she said, and walked the two steps to the garbage can. "Why is it so hard to eat the food we buy? Why do I feel like congratulating people when we actually do?"

"Juárez is a border town," I told her, shrugging at her questions because, really, are there answers? "Across the Rio Grande. Mixed up with the southern Rocky Mountains. It was the Mexican capital a long time ago, back during the Mexican Revolution."

Mom had an old slice of blueberry pie in her hand—a crusty plate of solidified slime somehow forgotten by Kev. She carried it to the sink and set it down. She turned to look at me. She looked as if she might never eat again.

"I atlas'ed Juárez," I said. "At Riley's." I knew she'd like that—me starting with a book as opposed to The Machine, which is what she called the internet. I figured that that small fact would help my cause.

"Well, that's all terrific, Georgia. But I still don't get why you'd want to go to Juárez. There's a whole wide, explorable world out there. If you're going anywhere, that is."

"I got the idea from a flyer," I said.

"You're being sketchy here, Georgia. Frustratingly vague." She smiled, but it was a tired smile. She had a bag of wilted lettuce in her hands. Above our heads, a rumble had started. We heard Geoff first: "Cut it out."

"GoodWorks," I said, rushing to explain before the next inevitable explosion. "It's this—I don't know—organization, I guess. It collects teens from here and takes them down there for community improvement projects."

"I see." She frowned, and the two dark valleys between her eyebrows deepened. Upstairs, Kev was yelling Geoff's name. Now he was running down the hall so fast that the light fixture above us shook. "Frankly, it sounds a little impulsive, Georgia. Make sure, before you go any further, that this is what you want." Mom might have said more, but the phone began ringing, and she cut across the room to get it.

I felt myself growing anxious—that hurt in my chest, that knot at my throat. I filled my lungs with air, closed my eyes, let the air go. Sometimes I could stop anxieties from getting nasty that way—sideline the attacks from their own game, breathe them right out of my mind. Mom on the phone was saying, "Oh, no. I'm so sorry." She was walking out of the kitchen to take the news alone. Another Kev crisis, I figured. Kev, who was upstairs yelling from behind a closed door and who always managed to mess with the day.

A few minutes later I was back up in my room—door shut, computer on, in the middle of a Google. I was humming to block out the noise of my older brother and then my cell phone rang. It was Riley, talking before

I even said hello. That was one of Riley's things—so much effervescing talk, when she wanted to talk, that Ms. Jean from school had dubbed her Bubbles. I called her that sometimes, when I was trying to get her attention.

"So, like, I swear this happened: She screwed up the self-tanner." Riley chirped, she couldn't help herself. She was a fast-talking, pitch-perfect soprano.

"Who? Your mom?"

"Of course my mom. Who else could screw up a self-tanner?"

Anyone, I thought. But no one else Riley'd notice.

"So I hear this noise, and I think the water pipes are broken; but it was her, the way she was crying. I've never heard my mother cry like that, and you know how she's had some crying doozies—you've seen her."

"Crying over a tan gone wrong?"

"She had little anklets of orange above her feet, you know? Like a henna tattoo or something."

"She told you that?" The truth is, I rarely saw Riley's mother sit down and tell her only child anything. They could be together without being together, the negatives in each other's equations. Riley's mom was the most disappointed person I ever knew. Always someone somewhere had it better: A bigger house. A buffer husband. A bound-for-fortunes daughter.

"No. I saw it," Riley was saying. "I'd gone into her room to find out what was wrong—I thought maybe she was hurt or something, maybe she needed some actual help, maybe I could be *useful*—right, yeah, what a concept—and the door to her dressing room was open. I found her in there trying on shoes with just her underwear on, all bawling over her self-tanner mistake."

"Why not just put on a pair of socks and forget about it?" I asked.

"She and Dad are going out. You know. To a *function.*"

"Oh." I got a picture of Riley's mother in my head—her skimpy little skirts and low-cut sleeveless sweaters. The ultragigantic diamond ring that she wore on the ring finger of her right hand that looked more like a weapon than like jewelry.

"I told her she should go with a pair of lace-up sandals, and I wasn't even being sarcastic, I swear. I thought lace-up sandals could help, thought it was a genius solution. But you know what she did right then, when I was talking? She slammed her dressing-room door in my face and told me to mind my own business." Riley laughed, but I could tell she wasn't feeling funny; she always laughed hardest when things were bad.

"She's so hysterical, my mother," Riley said. "She just is." She kept laughing again, and I held on, listening. I didn't press, because I never did. To be Riley's best friend back then was to give Riley room. It meant being best-in-class at standing back. "Slammed the door in my face," Riley repeated. "You gotta love my mom."

"Sorry, Ri," I said. "That sucks."

"What about you?" she asked at last. "What's up with the smart girl?"

"Googling Juárez," I told her.

"What about that Lit thing you had due?"

"Got Lit under control," I lied. "But Juárez I don't. It's a complicated place."

"They call winter break a break for a reason," Riley said. "You're supposed to be taking it easy."

The thing is, I'm truly terrible at taking it easy. I have a habit of piling things on and wanting things to be perfect and going out of my way to make things harder than they are. It's not that I'm running toward success so much as trying to keep my big wide feet off the heartbreak path of failure, and I don't even know why I ended up this way—I can't blame my parents or the example of my brothers.

I was the kind of kid who thought you had to color inside the lines—that if you missed and your crayon strayed, you had done bad; you were wrong. I'd practiced my handwriting until my fingers hurt, thinking that my letters had to match the ones in books. I'd put only the perfect shells from the Stone Harbor shore into my neon orange bucket, then stand with the hose on the gravel beside the beach house, scrubbing the sand from the shells. I'd perfected a technique on the monkey bars so that I'd always make it across without fail. I still picked up my room without being told, and that way my mom could apply all her reminding skills to my wreck-making brothers. Once, in second grade, when Mrs. Kalin asked the entire class to write the words *I will be quiet when the teacher is talking* twenty times in a row on blue-lined paper, she'd exempted me on account of my being so freakishly well-behaved, attentive. I remember being jealous of the other kids that day. Jealous and aware of my grave difference.

So that when I found the flyer about Juárez, I had to know about Juárez—whatever I could find, whatever sources. The atlas, the library, and, at home, my good friend Google, which is like falling down an endless hole—you could spend every waking hour chasing question marks with Google. I typed in the word and all these portals came up; and the more I read, the more confusing Juárez got, the more impossible to squeeze within a box.

For example: There are a lot of people who have passed through Juárez—famous people, rich people, smugglers. People trying to get out and people trying to get in, the traffic going both ways across the river's bridges. I liked the name of that river: Rio Grande. I liked how the river defined the edges not just of cities but of countries. There's El Paso and there's Juárez, and there's the river in between them. The fish must be citizens of both.

Meanwhile, the last battle of the Mexican Revolution was fought in Juárez. Meanwhile, John Wayne and Elizabeth Taylor and Steve McQueen sat drinking in Club Kennedy, a bar; and once Charles Lindbergh stopped by; and sometimes they'll film a movie in Juárez, when they want that whole, authentic Wild West feel. Every time I Googled Juárez, I found out something new; but every single time, also, I found myself reading about the *muertas*. About those young women—hundreds of them—who'd gone missing. They weren't much older than me, and some were younger than me; they'd go off to school or work and not come home. Later, in the desert, the women would be found: brutalized, dead, and abandoned. The country had been on a manhunt for a serial killer ever since 1993, but no such monster had been found. Tori Amos had written a song. Human rights groups protested. Still, young women from families without means up and disappeared.

The *muertas* stories were always right there in my research on Juárez, near as a mouse click. They always made me sadder than I can say—not afraid of Juárez, but sad for Juárez, full of some big desire to do something that would make things better for the ones the murders left behind. I'd read the stories until I couldn't anymore, then stand up and walk away. Go down the hall and outside and through the front door and either north, toward the horse show grounds, or south, where the older houses with their trembling gardens cast dark, moist shadows late at night. I needed stars and moon and night air, so I walked—worrying about women I'd never know; thinking about all that can't be changed or controlled; trying to envision Juárez, this place of complications and contradictions, where perfect, I pretty quickly figured out, wasn't the issue: Survival was. Survival under a hot sun, along a tired river, among factory jobs that paid hardly enough to sustain a family, and also among unsolved murders and loss.

In Juárez all my little self-imposed rules would be tested, the things I tried to control, my minuscule attempts at doing most things right. I'd be a rising senior that summer, on the verge of college. I needed a release from the narrow outlines of my life.

But it's not as if I understood this at first, in the days just after finding the flyer. All I knew then was that I had grown desperate for some kind of change in view. Desperate for a way to heal myself from the panic attacks that I had not told a soul about, the panic attacks that also seemed like failure. Even Riley, my only longtime best friend, didn't know what I went through. But then again, she was keeping secrets, too. We were each hiding demons from the other.

That night we waited until Dad got home to call Good-Works and ask questions. Mom dialed the kitchen phone first, then Dad and I picked up—me in the upstairs hall, Dad in the living room, Mom taking the lead. She interrogated. Dad clarified. Mack, the leader of this GoodWorks trip, answered every question calmly. They were looking for a dozen local teens who wanted to make a different kind of difference, Mack said. Teens who could recognize the value of small steps in vast places. This trip would focus on a *colonia* called Anapra, where the people by and large were good—working at jobs that paid some fifty dollars a week, struggling for food, struggling for water, struggling for survival in their sixty-square-foot houses. GoodWorks was liaising with a local outfit, Mack said, an organization whose sole business and purpose was to give American teens the chance to get to know the real people of Anapra and to leave something lasting in their wake. "These trips change lives," Mack said, and my mom was quiet. "They change perceptions on both sides of the border."

"Safety," Dad said, "is a concern."

"We take every precaution," Mack said.

"It's a complicated world," Mom said.

"There are no guarantees," Mack agreed. "None in Juárez, none in any city in the world. But we have history on our side at GoodWorks. A long-running program with an impeccable safety profile. As for the health of those who go: We require up-to-date inoculations, including hepatitis A. We're zealous about water supplies and dehydration."

"What about housing?" I asked. I wanted to be able to picture the whole thing, to visualize two weeks away.

"We're still working some of that out," Mack said. "We'll have all our plans in place by our first kickoff meeting, which we'll hold in February."

That night I could hear my parents talking late. The next morning I found a note slipped beneath my door: *Honey, if you want to go, you can.* It was written in my father's hand. My mom had drawn a heart for love.

It was early. The skies were gray. There was a crack

of sun low on the horizon, but there'd soon be a lashing of cold winter rain. I took a good look around my room—at the wallpaper I'd chosen when I was seven, at the mobile of butterflies that I had never bothered taking down, at all the English springer spaniel porcelains my dad had given me once as gifts because we could never get a real dog of our own—Geoff was allergic. It looked, in my room, as if nothing ever happened. But something had to happen, that was the thing, if I was to rise above all the mounds of worry that were threatening to do me in.

I picked up my cell and turned it on. I called Riley, who never turned her own phone off. "Hey," I said after she'd said hello.

"Georgia," she moaned, "what are you doing? It's not even—like, what time is it, Georgia?" She yawned. I could hear her rustling around in her bed.

"Listen," I said.

"I'm listening."

"Ri, you're going to Juárez, right? You're going to come?" I was sitting on my bed, wearing a T-shirt and a pair of Old Navy shorts. I was sitting there, and then I stood and walked over to the window and looked out at the little-kid swing set in the yard—still there as if my parents thought we kids would stay little forever.

"I have to ask my mother, Georgia." Riley's voice was small, the opposite of effervescent. That was the thing about Riley. She could be so back and forth. "It's going to freak her out."

"When are you going to ask?"

"I don't know. Maybe today, when she's nursing her hangover." The thought of this made Riley laugh. And then she couldn't stop laughing. Her laughter picked up speed, gained force.

"You have to go because you want to go," I heard myself saying. "Not because you want to freak your mother out."

"Yeah, I guess," Riley said, growing quiet again. My bedroom windows were beginning to streak with rain. Tomorrow, the third quarter of school would begin.

three

They like to tell you that panic attacks begin in your head. My first began and ended with my heart.

I'd piled on too much at school, but it was not as if that was news. It was my sophomore year, and I'd stacked AP Biology next to Honors Spanish next to Trig; but it was AP English that took the cake for messing with my head. *Nuance* was Mr. Buzzby's favorite word, and into every assignment he would wedge his famous shades of gray. He asked for lines, for boundaries, for distinctions. He drove the whole class mad.

Some days we'd walk in and there'd be paired terms on the board: *Insidious/Invidious. Ominous/Onerous. Nom de plume/Nom de guerre. Tortuous/Torturous.* "You have ten minutes," he'd say, "to write an essay delineating the proper use of each word." Mr. Buzzby balanced his frameless glasses on the end of his nose. He combed his cantaloupe-colored hair straight back. He tacked his knitted ties with a silver pin, and his face never evolved from a frown. The twinned terms were only ever ten-point essays, but there was no predicting them. You walked in. You sat down. There were the words on the board, Buzzby's frown on his face, the relentless clock on the wall. Sometimes I had something to say and sometimes I didn't, and when I didn't, my heart would start pounding. I'd sit at my desk holding my Uni-ball above an empty page, listening to the clock's minute hand.

But that wasn't it. That was not what set the attacks in motion; that was just a case of nerdy nerves. My first veridical panic attack had come the day before the marking period ended, when an Objects at Rest essay was due. We had been studying Pablo Neruda. We had read his words out loud: "It is very appropriate, at certain times of day or night, to look deeply into objects at rest." Mr. Buzzby had given us a week to write eight "inspired" pages—something, Mr. Buzzby said, that would make the Chilean poet proud. I had a grading-period B that I had to pull up to an A. Or thought I did, because isn't that the way it is? The colleges we choose not choosing us unless we've proven our utter readiness?

I'd had what I'd thought was a brilliant idea: Object at rest equals Kev when he is sleeping. I didn't doubt it, didn't second-guess it—just had the idea and blasted through. I'd stolen into my brother's room at night and sat in that strange silence. I paid attention to the sound of stillness—to its color, to the rays of moonlight that plashed against my brother's sheets. "Kev at Rest," that's what I called my essay; and when it was finally done, when I'd gone to sleep the night before it was due, I felt as though I'd trumped the assignment and earned myself an AP English A. I was on top of things, where people expected me to be, which is what I expected of myself.

I'd woken up dying. I'd woken up pinned to the bed by a bolt of pain, with a heart split wide and bloody.

There was no feeling, nothing, in my left arm. There wasn't any air in my lungs. I was flattened and ashed, and when I tried calling out, not one word appeared; when I pounded at my headboard with my right fist, nobody came. I was fifteen years old and a bleating terror: I'd never drive, I'd never kiss, I'd never grow up and leave my ransacked teenaged self behind.

I was dying all because Kev was no object: My heart had figured that out. He was a living, breathing human being, pain in the butt that he usually was, and my essay was wrong, my A was an F, my body was blaring, *You're done for.* I love it when people think you can talk yourself out of pain. You can't. You can only defend yourself against it; and to defend yourself, you have to muscle up. You have to face your fears and pulp them. You have to fight until there isn't one fear left.

You have to get perspective.

Winter couldn't summon snow. I'd have given anything for a couple of white days off, but the temperature hovered in the mid-thirties and the clouds could manage only rain. Most of the days were gray all the way through, and on the few days when the sun shone brightly, the mercury in the thermometers plunged. The atmosphere was doing a lousy job of getting its snow act together.

By February of the year of Juárez, the seniors were already hyped about the internships they'd start in May—Jeremy getting a gig at Wired 96.5, Josh writing a screenplay under the wing of someone famous, Haley returning to the elementary school, where she'd assist with the third graders. They'd tell us their big news at lunch or in between classes in the halls. Pretty soon, too, the college gossip was flying: who'd gotten into where and who hadn't and all the guessing about why, all the talk about whether there still might be time to shine up our own junior résumés a bit. The seniors were free; they'd been let loose from their shackles. I envied them that. Geoff, too, had been liberated, had gotten his ticket to S. I. Newhouse at Syracuse. The best communications program in the country, Mom said, something of which the whole family should be proud. Even Kev high-fived Geoff when the news came in. Even he sat with us and watched the DVD that came with the acceptance letter.

But for us juniors, for me, there were only exams

on the horizon, AP tests, a second shot at the SATs, on which I'd done better than I had thought I'd do but where there was always room, as my counselor said, for some meaningful improvement. Riley acted as if it didn't matter then and would matter never—took the SATs once and shrugged at her scores. "Whatever," she said, and that was it. She said the most exciting thing about planning for college was imagining all the fabulosity that'd come with living away from home. She was looking for exits, even in winter. It was my fault, not understanding how genuinely desperate she was to disappear.

You get caught up, junior year, in yourself. You can't help it. There's that much pressure.

By the middle of February, Mack had collected a gang of eleven, and even though it wasn't his perfect dozen, he'd scheduled a first actual meeting on a Thursday at the local GoodWorks office some twenty minutes down the road. All of us had at least one parent with us; that was one of Mack's rules: It's a family thing. Maybe it's the kids who are flying south, but everyone commits to the mission and Dad was my family rep that day.

So there we were, in the bottom-wedge office space that had been leased to GoodWorks for cheap by a corporate sponsor. Instead of windows there were color photocopies of photos from prior-year excursions. A well-water project in Nicaragua, Mack said, rapping his finger against the pinned-to-the-wall pic. A roof raising in Honduras. Soil work in El Salvador, where some of the coffee farming was going organic. Every year a brand-new hillside or neighborhood, a brand-new start. Little seeds, Mack called them. We plant them, get them started. The communities take everlasting care.

Mack had a carousel projector with him—one of those old-fogy kinds. He made the room dark and then beamed the thing on, and for every face or mound or hill of beans that shone through the black-blue-white light, he had a story. Transformations, he called them. He said that no initiative was its own foregone conclusion. That success in the end was not just the what that was tried but the who that had attempted. I looked around. Except for Riley, these kids, to me, were one hundred percent strangers—a few from private schools, a few from competing public high schools, a handful of seniors from my own Rennert High with whom I'd never had reason to mix. We wore name tags around our necks, our school names on the line below our names. Our parents sat at our sides, too well dressed, too manicured, a little shaken in a room of walls bruised blue, black, and white with poverty.

Riley was turning the bracelets on her wrist. When Mack stopped the show and flipped the overhead lights back on, her mother was the first with a question. "I'm assuming they'll be nice—the accommodations?" she asked, no doubt expecting a Hilton. I felt my mouth twist up into a half-smiled smirk. I crossed my arms and awaited Mack's answer.

"We'll be living in a church," he said, looking at me so that I'd know he hadn't forgotten my question of several weeks ago. "We'll be taking a one-hour drive each day to the site of the squatters' village. We rent the vans in El Paso."

"Are there beds in this church?" Riley's mother persisted, her voice in a pinch.

"We ask everyone to bring sleeping bags," Mack said. "We prepare ourselves for all seasons, for beds or no beds, for rain or shine."

Riley's mother had one of those hairstyles that hugged the face and then flipped out, like the bottom half of an *S*. She had the fingers of one hand in her hair now, telegraphing not so much nerves as disdain. She could have asked about the vans, the roads, the existence or not of roofs, the people of Juárez, the ways in which they struggled. Instead, she asked about the bathrooms.

Mack was used to this, you could tell—his face grizzled by a lifetime of summers in the sun, his hair dark beneath streaks of blond that, I guessed, he'd had painted there. He had lovely green-brown eyes, Mack did. His eyes were how I guessed that he was young. Or not old, anyway. Maybe close to thirty.

"I see," Riley's mother said.

"This reminds me of a cardinal rule in Juárez," Mack said. "No flushing paper of any kind down the toilets. You do, and you spoil a whole neighborhood's plumbing. You do, and they come looking for the person who perpetrated the toilet crime."

"Yeah. But," said this girl who called herself Jazzy. Exotic, with long, dark, crinkling hair.

"No buts on this one." Mack didn't even let her get

started. "You throw it in, you fish it out. That is the way it gets done."

I saw the girl named Sophie turn a pale shade of green, which looked particularly odd against her bright red hair. I heard Riley start to shake her head, the tambourines going off down her ear. "I owe you big-time for this," she leaned over and said.

"At your service." I smiled at her. "Always."

One hour later, the eleven of us kids plus the chaperones plus the parents who would stay behind while their children planted seeds straggled out into the bright sunshine of a cold, blue February day where a quarter-moon already pressed into the sky. Those of us who were new to one another did the limp handshake thing, exchanged phone numbers and email addresses, said we'd friend one another on Facebook. Our parents hurried us along. As soon as we got into his car and closed the doors, my dad, who had all along been keeping his own close counsel, said, "You know you don't absolutely have to go."

"I know," I said, looking at him, his fine broad face, his graying temples. "That's the best part."

"What is?"

"The chance to choose to do something like this."

"As opposed to?"

"Being required. Going around thinking that you had to."

"I'm surprised Riley's mom hasn't signed up as chaperone," he said after deciding, I guess, not to press not going too hard. Turning for an instant, he caught my eye and smiled. He was in on my jokes about Mrs. Marksmen, which was just one of the millions and millions of reasons that he ranked high on my list of great guys.

"No room for all her face creams," I said. "No time for morning Pilates."

"Let's not tell your mom about all the driving—not yet."

"I know," I said. "I thought of that."

"Let's tell your mom some of the transformation stories. We can probably score with that."

four

My second panic attack had happened right out in broad daylight, forty miles away from here, at Longwood Gardens. The place is one-thousand-plus acres gigantic, with forty total gardens, indoor and out. Sometimes we go there in the summer for the lighted fountain shows. Sometimes we go in winter for the Christmas holiday lights and poinsettias. But this had been Easter week of my sophomore year, and my little brother was bored. After the long, tedious winter, my mother, too, wanted out. "We could try Longwood," she had said that morning at breakfast, as if we were all on the executive council. Geoff said no thank you, but what would you expect of Geoff, who had, for as long as I could remember, lived his life outside the circle of our family? Kev and I piled into the car.

It was one of those days. Half the sky was blue and half was floated through with puffed cloud matter. When the clouds covered the sun, it was perfect sweater weather. When the sun was bare, it felt as if nothing could go wrong. Just past the entrance gates at Longwood the parking lot is huge. Once you've parked and paid and walked past the gift shop through the tunnel, the gardens fall off in all directions—toward the conservatory; toward the Peirce-duPont House; toward a bell tower, a waterfall, a theater; toward gardens. Kev didn't have a destination in mind. He wanted your basic runaround.

"Do you mind, Georgia?" my mother asked, and I shrugged and said it'd be all right. I'd let Kev spin out some of his energy—that was the plan—and then we'd all meet at the café at one, when Mom would let me go to the orchids alone while she plied Kev with yellow-mustarded hot dogs.

But Kev took off before I could tell him not to, and

so now I was running too—down the alley between the Topiary and Rose Garden, then past the Rose Garden toward Forest Walk, where the tulip trees were colossal beasts, too big, even, for Longwood. It was early for lilacs, but as I ran I noticed a few clusters getting ready to bloom. I noticed, too, that Kev's red shoelaces had come undone, but he was too far down the long stretch of the Flower Garden Walk for me to do anything about it. I called to him, but he wouldn't hear me. "Kev!" I pleaded, but he was gone toward the fountains and the Peony Garden and the huge Meadow that lay beyond the rest of it—a field that seemed to have no edges, that just went on and on. There were paths that crossed and vanished. There was shade, then there was sun. The problem was that Kev could run anywhere, and I was doing nothing to thwart him.

"Hey," I asked a guy who looked as if he might work at Longwood. "Did some kid just run by here?"

"Blond?" he said. "A girl?"

"No. A boy. Red shoelaces? Curly hair?"

The guy stood and thought before he shook his head no and wished me luck. But a miracle was what I needed. Luck never cut it with Kev.

Maybe someday we'll all be standing around the track cheering for my breakneck brother. Maybe we'll be saying, "Remember when?" But that day I wished I'd doped up the kid's sneakers with lead. I wished I had a chain and he was tethered to it. Running, I had to strategize on the fly—choose a path he might be on, change course when I couldn't find him. "Kev!" I kept calling, but he never answered. Finally I asked a woman with a stroller. "My kid brother," I said, and I tried to explain. When she said no, she hadn't seen him, I asked an old man who'd come along. I couldn't keep the awful possibility of the Meadow from my thoughts, for if Kev had gone that far and had started down that path, chances were I'd never find him. Chances were I'd have to wait for my brother to find me, and Kev never does take initiative.

Panic, I'm telling you, begins in the heart. Panic is big buzzard wings banging wretched and trapped against the bones of your ribs, knocking your windpipe loose, swiping your logic. Panic makes you stupid when you have to be smart. It makes you stop in your tracks when what you must do right then is run. I lost my brother at Longwood Gardens for an hour that day, and in the midst of my chase I lost myself. I can't even tell you what happened next, except that I was sobbing, hardly breathing by the time I saw him—Kev sauntering his way toward me on the path, his hair like a rooster crest on the top of his sweaty head.

"Jesus, G., what's with you?" he said. Then we went to find the café. Kev didn't care at all that I'd been scared, just thought I was being big-sister weird; and it would have done neither of us one bit of good to explain to our mom what had just happened. You can feel as if you're dying when you're inside a panic attack. Then, when you realize you'll probably survive, the red, hot, sizzled part of you just wants to run and hide.

It's no good trying to explain panic after the fact. It wouldn't have helped to get my parents involved, or at least I couldn't see how. I could only fix myself. I was old enough to have figured that out.

The day after Mack's meeting, my cell performed its faithful "You're Beautiful" ring tone. I flipped it open to Riley. "Oh my God," she was saying before I'd even said hey. "My mother," she continued. "She's *worse* than a freak show."

My mom and dad were out—some charity event. I'd finally gotten Kev through his homework by turning it into a game, giving him a penny for every math problem he solved. Geoff was upstairs and online, Facebooking with the Syracuse crowd. Even if he was hardly one of us anymore, even if in his mind Geoff had long since moved on, Kev still had the power to annoy him. To march him straight back into the circle of family.

"So, in the car back, she's, like, not even speaking, right?" Riley was saying. "My mother—all dumbstruck. Like *that's* normal. Then we get to a mile from here and she says, 'No daughter of mine,' then goes totally flabbergasted, speechless. 'Mom? Are you all right?' I ask her. And she says—and I mean, this was her big moment, Georgia—'Hygiene, Riley. It's so important.' And I say, 'Hygiene, Mom? Hygiene?' As if I still go around wearing embroidered pinafores and patent leather slippers. As if she hasn't figured out that dirt is not the world's worst evil."

"Sounds like she blocked the transformation stories."

"I guess."

"But it doesn't matter, right? Because you're the one who's going."

"I guess." And here Riley paused the way she can when she's balancing the scales of justice in her mind. "I guess so. Yeah." She was so up and down. So hot and cold. There was no Riley middle.

"What?" I said.

"Nothing, really," she answered. "It's just . . . Do you still think, Georgia, that we should go? I mean, after the presentation and everything? We won't know anyone but each other. Not at first, at least. It sounds more like work than like fun."

"Picture the summer without Juárez," I said. "What do you see?"

"Windows down, air conditioner on, ear buds in. Anything that I want is mine."

"And?" I pressed.

"Pretty," she said.

"*Too* pretty," I said. "Think about it." Kev had made his way upstairs. I took the phone around to the foyer so that I'd be near if there was trouble. Once Kev had come shooting around the spiral stairs headfirst, like an earthbound rocket. Once I'd found him trying to slide down the big oak banister. Once I'd found him urging a friend to leap for the crystal chandelier. *I will if you will,* I had heard him dare.

"It's going to be hot in Juárez," Riley said.

"That's a fact." I took a cautionary glance up at the stairs.

"We're going to hate the toilets."

"They'll be gross."

"We're going to be sleeping next to a bunch of kids we hardly know in a beat-up church in an across-the-border country. And then there's the fact of those *muertas.*" For at the meeting Mack had spoken of them; he had laid bare the facts. He'd said that in Anapra we would be among the families who had lost sisters and daughters to a wave of crime that wasn't entirely in check. "We'll be part of the healing," he'd said. Then he'd moved on, giving no one much time at all to dwell.

"You come up with some of the wackiest ideas," Riley said.

"I'm going to go, Ri. You go if you want to."

She was silent; I waited through her silence. "Seeds" is what she said at last, and then she started to laugh.

Upstairs, Kev was banging on Geoff's door and Geoff was telling him to quit. Now Kev was yelling at Geoff, and Kev was calling for me, and Ri was back inside silence.

"We're going to Juárez" is what she finally said. Definitive and certain.

"Both of us?"

"Yeah."

"Cool," I said, a single, grateful syllable.

"And tomorrow we go shopping."

"Shopping?"

"For the wardrobe," she said. "The Juárez trousseau."

"You're as crazy as your mom," I said.

She laughed. "Not even a possibility, Georgia."

five

You can't ride a bike to the mall from where I live. You have to wait for a ride. My mom did the drop-off; Riley's mom would collect. Within a year both of us would have our licenses. It was Saturday morning, and the place was mobbed. I felt like the Hulk beside Riley, who seemed even smaller than usual, all belted into her father's old Brooks Brothers shirt and her legs sheened over with spandex. She had kept her spangled sunglasses on. She'd painted another streak of orange into her hair—a broad stripe, like a hair band. She had on a pair of giraffey-tall shoes that had the skinniest, most impractical heels.

Spring break was a week away. A man wearing a big-eared bunny suit was passing tinfoiled chocolates to the shopping clientele, the same man, I swear, who does Santa. I took two of the eggs off his furry paw, said thank you to the piece of mesh that only half disguised his face. Riley took precisely none.

"They're *free*," I said, imploring.

She wasn't tempted. I peeled away the tinfoil from the chocolates, one by satisfying one. "Best chocolate on the planet," I said, exaggerating.

"Then take another," Riley said. Which made me feel like the Hulk Times Two, and made her seem even smaller. I minded, a lot, that she wouldn't eat the chocolate. I minded the thought that crept in. Riley was too small. Some part of me knew it. Another part of me didn't want to know.

"You're a royal pain in the butt, Marksmen," I told her.

"I'm concentrating," she said.

And she was. Because we'd come to the court in the middle of the mall; there were choices in every direction. You could go east or you could go west or you could keep on going north, which would take you to a bridge that floated you high over a sea of parked Beamers. On the other side of the bridge you'd find a second, newer shopping complex that was linked, way beyond, to a brand-new third. I always got to this court and its spoked-out choices and ached, all of a sudden, to give it up and get myself home. Riley, though, was a master navigator. She had the blueprint of the mall and all its stores imprinted on her brain, kept running lists in her head. I let her think for both of us, on behalf of the Juárez trousseau, on behalf of my not thinking about why she was too small.

"I have it all figured out," she said now, hiccuping a little laugh, adjusting the glasses on her nose.

I rolled the chocolate foils into two tiny aluminum balls and tossed them into the nearest metal can. "Don't worry. I'm not asking questions."

Everything is polished to smoothness in the mall—the granite floors, the skylights, the panes of glass, the music that falls from you can't tell where—and the weather is always mid-May—perfectly perfect. Riley and I were with the mob and against the mob, around and down and through, until we found our way to a boutique named Diamonds, which was narrow and dark beyond its glass front and abundant inside with stacked, racked things. Diamonds was a shop for girls our age, all trends and tightness; and that meant, of course, that it was flooded with mothers—with women whose number one m.o. was to outyouth their daughters.

"Isn't that Lauren Carmichael's mom?" Riley whispered into my ear as we walked in; and I said, "Oh my God, it is," because there she was, Lauren's mom, posing in front of the three-way mirror in a little spring kilt and cut-to-the-naval blouse. She had a Cleopatra necklace at her throat and a couple of platinum chains around one ankle; and if she'd had to bend down to, say, strap on some sandals, we'd have seen what you never want to see of a full-grown woman's rear end.

"Pretty," Riley muttered, pushing her shades up off her eyes now and planting them firmly over her new orange stripe, behind her ears.

"They should keep to their own stores," I said.

"You should tell that to my mother," Riley confided. "Once, I swear, she was in here when I was, trying on some real low capris with a lacy sort of a tee.

She didn't even see me; that's how self-absorbed she was. Couldn't take her eyes off the mirror."

I rolled my eyes. "There should be laws," I said.

Riley laughed, one of her best, big, out-loud laughs, then turned and started sorting through the racks, piling herself up with whatever she might want until she was cascaded with clothes.

"You want me to hold some of that?" I offered.

"Nope," she huffed. "I got it."

"You want me to, like, get you something else?"

"Georgia," she said. "Georgia, Georgia. Why don't you think about yourself for once? Look around. Pick out something nice. Go back there. Try it on."

"I'm not the Diamonds kind of girl," I said.

"You could be," she said, "if you wanted."

"Right." I picked up something red and sheer and low-cut and clingy and pressed it to myself. I traded that for something flouncy. I pulled one of those two-inch sweaters off a shelf. "I'm being strictly God honest," I said. "How gross would I look in all that?"

"I thought we were going to a thing called Transformations." Behind all her prospective clothes, Riley was starting to sound exasperated.

"The world, Riley. We're transforming the world."

"And where is it, again, that you live?"

"The world." I blushed. "I guess."

"So get with the program. Start with yourself."

"I think you're missing the point here, Riley."

"You are such a *dose*," she said, but she was smiling. And then she was backing away and turning a corner until I couldn't see her anymore. She'd disappeared behind a changing-room door. I could hear the clattering of hangers, the whooshing of clothes, the riptide sound of zippers. I went over to where she was. On the other side of the door, the commotion continued but Riley herself was bizarrely quiet.

"Hey," I said after too much time had passed.

"Hey," she said back, her voice thin and distant.

"You okay back there?"

"Nothing fits," she said.

"Because you're too skinny," I said.

"No. Because I'm too fat."

I sighed real loud. It had to be a joke.

But Riley wasn't laughing. She was clattering with the hangers again. She was banging things around, fitting her feet into her shoes, opening the door to the changing room. She'd thrust her sunglasses back down to her nose. The orange stripe around her head looked flushed and oddly disturbed.

"Let's just get out of here," Riley said, pushing past me now. "Okay?"

"Riley," I said. "Riley?"

"I'm serious," she said.

"I got that," I said.

I had to take a running start to catch her. There wasn't time to say what I was thinking.

six

The next day I waited for Riley to call. She didn't.

I called her three times.

She didn't answer.

seven

Two days later, Riley was, apparently, Riley. She had gotten to school before I had and pulled a beaded bracelet through the handle of my locker—beads like crystals, like little aquamarine chips that had been wired together in however many rows of five across. It was a Riley Special, fitted with a clasp. I put it on before I dialed my combo. Between third and fourth periods I saw her down the hall from me, caught inside a hurricane crowd. I raised my arm and the bracelet flashed. I'm sure I heard her laugh.

That afternoon I was hardly home when "You're

Beautiful" started singing. I threw my backpack down on the family room floor, then flew up the stairs, past Kev's room and into my own. I said hello and flopped onto my bed. Riley said hi and I smiled.

"Great bracelet," I told her.

"Yeah." She was slightly out of breath.

"It's not even my birthday, you goof. Or any other holiday that I remember."

"I made the bracelet," she said, "in anticipation of Juárez."

"I should have guessed."

"I'm making bunches."

My thoughts tried to go where Riley's had already been. "For the squatter girls?" I guessed.

"Won't it be fab? They'll be our hello-how-are-you presents."

I got a picture in my head of all those crystals in the sun. Of Riley, swirled by a knot of girls, doling out fashion north-of-the-border style. Of Riley, thin as a sunbeam. "How many are you making?" I asked.

"As many as I can." She seemed so pleased, so tipping close, again, to laughter.

"Mighty fine of you."

"I'm that kind of fine person."

"And generous."

"My mom buys the beads. I just string them."

"So, everything else is okay?" I asked. "You're fine?" I thought maybe I could get her to talk about the mall—maybe I could lead her there, general questions tiptoeing toward the correct, specific ones; and yes, I know, I should have asked more, pressed harder about why her sweetness that day had suddenly gone sour. About what she'd seen in the mirror. About how she *felt*. About what the hell she was doing to herself. But Riley was acting like the old, regular Riley. Seemed so happy with her jewelry diplomacy plans that I let things be, pretended to believe her when she said, "Things could not be finer. And you?"

"Preparing myself for the afternoon onslaught."

"The what?"

"Kev," I said, "will be home in half an hour."

"At least there's noise in your house."

"Noise?"

"The only noise here is my echo."

"Where's your mom?"

"Wherever she goes to get Botoxed."

"Where's your dad?"

"Wherever he can make himself some real-fast Botox cash."

"You can come over here, you know," I said, though I had a paper to write, and Kev would be back any second, and Geoff was already in his room, the door to which he'd pinned with a sign: STAY OUT OF HERE, KEVIN. I'M SERIOUS. The afternoons were hardly ever mine, and Riley knew it, but still she was there on her phone, talking to my phone, hanging on. Suddenly there was something sad right there despite her seeming happiness—her sarcasm, which was her favorite cover.

I rolled off the bed and squinched my phone between my ear and shoulder. I started unpacking the books from my backpack. Stacking them up on my desk in a minitower, waiting for Riley to go on.

"Georgia?" she said at last, softly, as if worried someone beside me would hear.

"Yeah?"

"Sorry for being a jerk."

"You're not a jerk."

"I am sometimes and so are you, but I want to tell you something."

I stood straight up, balanced the phone on my shoulder. Walked toward the window and looked out upon the yard. *I'm a jerk?* I wanted to say, but I let it go; it wasn't the time for off-topic tangents. "Anything, Riley. I'm listening." I could see my reflection in the window glass. A little line of worry down my brow. I looked past me, to the sky, to the clouds, to a pack of blackbirds, all together like a gang. I looked until I didn't see a thing.

"A couple of weeks ago I heard my mother on the phone. She didn't know I was around, and she was talking about me. Like she does. You know how she does. She was sitting on that stool in the kitchen where she doesn't cook a thing, with the phone up to her ear. She was going on and on about some shopping spree, and it was funny at first, so I was eavesdropping from the stairs. And then she started saying stuff that I didn't want to hear, but I couldn't move, and I sat there, listening."

I closed my eyes so that I could picture everything—Riley's mother in the spotless kitchen that's big enough to feed a football team, Riley on the steps with her knees up to her chin. "What was she saying, Ri?"

"She was telling whomever that she couldn't believe that she'd ended up with a daughter like me."

"Couldn't have, Riley, couldn't have. I mean, that's just not even—," I started to say, but I knew Riley's mother. I knew what a self-centered, self-congratulating Botox queen she could be. "You must have heard her wrong. There are five miles between your kitchen and those stairs, at least, for one thing."

"There's nothing wrong with my ears, Georgia. Plus it's not even close to five miles."

"Did she say— What else did she say? Was she referring to something specific?"

"She said I was average, Georgia. *Average.* Like that was worse than ugly."

"You are not average, Riley. I swear to God." All of a sudden I felt so mad inside, so big, hard-fisted angry. I felt like taking my bike and pumping the streets between my house and Riley's—waiting for the Botox queen to show up at one of her million doors so that I could give her a piece of my mind.

"I don't want to be average, Georgia." Riley's voice was unconvinced, and tiny.

"You aren't. Not even slightly."

"I didn't tell her that I heard her, right? I didn't want her to know? I didn't want anyone to know, except—Georgia, I can't get it out of my mind. I wake up, and it's there every day. I walk around this house when my mother's gone, and it's like her words are here instead." Riley said it as if someone like me had to give someone like her permission to walk right past her mother's words.

"She probably didn't mean it," I said, lying because I had to, lying because that's what you sometimes do for your best friend. "She was probably just talking the way she does, because it's cool to her—the sound of her own voice—because she's got so many friends like herself who live to be impressed. Or maybe she was drinking, Riley. Maybe—"

"It was five in the afternoon," Riley interrupted. "My father wasn't home. She wasn't drinking, and I know she meant it. Think about it, Georgia: There she is, a perfect woman in a perfect house with a daughter she's labeled average. Even my art, Georgia—that doesn't count for her. An artist daughter is not what passes for cool on the Main Line. I don't give her anything to boast about, and what is my mother without boasting material? What does she live for but that?"

"It's sick and you know it, Riley."

"It's how she sees me."

"It's not how other people see you. Everybody I know wants to be your best friend."

"Yeah, well. That job is filled."

I felt my eyes fill up, my throat go hoarse. I didn't have a fixing thing to say. "You're a good person, Riley."

"Except for when I am a jerk."

"Yeah. But I still love you."

Her voice was getting smaller. She was disappearing again, into herself. "My bracelets await me," she said at last.

"They're going to be so fabulous."

"You'd better be wearing yours tomorrow." She sniffed, and then she laughed; and that laugh was always the sign with us. That laugh was Move on, Don't dwell, Think forward. That laugh was Please, don't ask again.

"Wouldn't think of doing elsewise," I told her. And I meant it, forever and ever.

eight

My third panic attack happened during second period, April 3, sophomore year, right in the middle of AP English. Mr. Buzzby had written the last third of a poem called "Laundry" on the board, and I had been given the job of explicating the enjambed lines, of saying how they advance the poem, an assignment about which Mr. Buzzby seemed excessively proud. He called me up to the front of the room. He made me read aloud:

Two years gone and still your hand
lifts over the notes we sang to ease you
home. Winter, and the dark had fallen

through. Your future then
was the tricking back
past time. The smell of laundry
hung to dry. The strand
of pearls you dared to buy.
The day your mother

died. Your future was your sight,
which had gone before you,
and your words,
eclipsed now, too,
and your hand lifting over the notes we sang,
as if we might go with you, touched.

"How is the tension advanced by the incomplete syntax of the lines?" he asked. "How does the poem change speed and meaning upon the successive rejets?"

There are those who love to think out loud—the

debate teamers, the Model UNers, most of the Young Democrats crowd. I respect that, even admire it, but I am not that kind of person. I'm the kind who raises her hand when she's sure she's right, after she's had a couple of seconds to think. With his enjambment assignment, Mr. Buzzby had given me no time. He'd asked the question. I'd blinked. I felt the big bird's wings start to flutter in my heart, my tongue stick like a boot deep in mud. I got hot and clammy and everything spun out, and nothing I could do got me on track. I just stood there looking like a blubbering fool while the whole classroom stared back.

"Great poem" is what I said, sitting down. Wanting to run, wanting to hide, so incredibly desperate to get out. There was a noose at my throat, and the rope kept tightening, and my heart kept banging, and I had no feeling in my arm, not a bit, and if someone had asked if they could help me, I wouldn't have answered them. *Everything's closing in*, I'd say, but they'd look around, they'd see the facts, they'd know that I was going crazy.

You can't let people think you're nuts. Not when you're in high school.

For the next meeting at GoodWorks, my mother dropped me off at the curb so that she could get Kev to T-ball. Mrs. Marksmen, however, was not to be denied another round of turning up her perfect nose at bathroom and bunking scenarios. Riley sat at one end of the table, beside me. Her mother sat at the other, near Mack, as if she could leverage her beauty against his raw reports and make everything first-rate dainty in Juárez.

She so missed the point. She so didn't know her only daughter. One daughter and no job. You'd have thought she could have gotten more right.

I watched her, I couldn't help it. I thought about how bizarrely doppelgängerish Riley and her mother were—the same slivered nose, the same wide cheeks, the same model-worthy jaw. Riley's mom had bleached her freckles. She'd had her forehead smoothed to silk by dried and purified botulinum toxin type A. She'd put everything she had into being beautiful, and Riley had committed exaggerations of her own—punching all those holes into her earlobe, striping her hair shades of neon sun and Mars red, painting her nails the color of some witch's brew. And yet, a perfect stranger would identify them as family. In a couple of years they would be confused for sisters. That particular day, in early May, Riley was wearing an extra-large T-shirt over a pair of baggy jeans. Her mother wore a skin-tight camisole and a waist-hugging, flared Gypsy skirt.

"The point is this," Mack was saying "We're not just there to help. We're there as emissaries of our country, exemplifying the best of America. Everything we do will be watched—what we wear, how we eat, how we are with one another, what we achieve, what we leave behind. Process is as important as outcomes here. The intangibles will weigh in against the facts."

"So, and, like . . ." It was Jazzy, wild Jazzy, waving her hand, taking the stage. "What exactly will we be doing once we're there? I mean, what seeds will we be planting?"

"Your question is my segue," said Mack. He stood and walked to the light switch, darkened the room. He turned our attention to that part of the wall that was empty of transformation pictures as he flicked on the ancient projector. An aerial map of Anapra came into view. A couple of word slides on landscape and topography that described how Anapra, the squatters' village at the edge of Juárez, slouched downward from some hills that were made of stone and crumbling to sand. Finally Mack got to Jazzy's question, a smile on his sun-creased face.

"Right here," he said, indicating the top of a hill with a pointer, "is a tiny community church, a community kitchen, the house where the community pastor and his family live, and also a soccer field, monkey bars. Between the buildings here"—he pointed—"is a narrow stretch of dry, white earth. It's there that we'll be putting up a bathroom."

"We're building a pastor's bathroom?" the kid named Corey asked.

"It will be the community's bathroom," said Mack.

"The *whole* community?" asked Mrs. Marksmen, whose face, so frozen smooth, could not express the shock her voice emitted. Riley caught a glimpse of the frozen look too. I heard her drop one flip-flop. Disgust, maybe. Or shame.

"Two toilet stalls for men and two for women," Mack explained. "A one-for-each shower on either side.

Running water for people who have little to none. A place of dignity and well-being beneath a sweltering sun." Mr. Buzzby would have called this oratory. Mack seemed delighted with himself—complete—and stopped.

"We're building a *bathroom*?" Sophie repeated, not to verify but to question the logic.

"In two weeks?" asked Sam. Sam had, it was clear, recently blonded his hair. Bright shoots of it flew off his head like comet tails.

"We'll be getting a bathroom facility under way," Mack clarified, with the practiced patience that comes from doing who knows how much time in his profession. "We'll level the land, pour the foundation, raise up the walls, hammer in a roof."

"And what happens when we leave?" I wondered aloud.

"We're planting seeds," Mack said. "Remember? After we leave, we trust the community to carry the momentum forward."

"Transformations," Riley murmured.

"Yes." Mack nodded. "Yes."

"But where"—it was Corey again—"do we get what we need in a place like this? I mean, two-by-fours? Nail guns? Concrete mixers? Where is all *that* supposed to come from?"

Mack walked to the wall again, snapped on the light. He was ready for the question. He distributed the stack of papers that had been sitting there before him all along—architectural sketches, a series of lists, a page crowded with addresses and maps, health forms, permission forms, another list, this one a checklist. All you could hear for a time was the sound of paper rustling, the sound of sighs, whispers over sighs. The quietest person in the room was the biggest person in the room—a guy with a boulder for a head and with shoulders as wide as North America. He had these incredibly lovely eyes, and thick black hair that had fallen down across his face. I don't think he moved so much as an eyelash. I looked at him, and then I looked down. The concrete would be hand mixed, I read. We'd each be bringing a hammer, a work apron, and gloves; we could forget about nail guns. A hardware store in El Paso would be providing the lumber, the cost of which was being covered by a sponsor. The pastor, who had helped to build a few buildings before, would oversee construction.

"Look." Riley banged her elbow into mine. I

registered the pain.

"What's that?"

"So much for our Juárez trousseau." She was pointing to a subsection on a page of lists titled "Attire." Beneath the heading were instructions about drawstring scrubs and slogan-free Ts, shoes with closed toes, no heels. "How very special," Riley muttered after I turned to glance at her.

"How not American," I whispered back, but not softly enough, evidently, for Mack heard me.

"Georgia raises a key point here," Mack announced, and all eyes went first to me before they trailed back up to him. I blushed. "When we're guests in a place like Juárez, we dial ourselves down," he said. "We project decency, and caring. No T-shirts advertising favorite rap artists or award-winning beer. No snug-fitting pants. No flashes of skin or of wealth. Wherever we go, we leave a mark. Wearing the right things is one of the ways we leave the right one."

"You're asking us to wear nurses' pants?" Jazzy demanded.

"You'll be grateful for the cotton in that heat," Mack said.

"Happy for T-shirts?" Jazzy whined.

"Better than spandex."

"And what about that heat?" Mrs. Marksmen asked in a tone that suggested that Mack should be doing something to fix it. "What about *that*?"

"We keep hydrated," he answered. "We wear sunblock."

Mrs. Marksmen shook her head. She gave me a look that practically pleaded *How could you?* Riley laughed into her hand. Her fingers were the skinniest and most girllike I'd ever seen; somehow I'd never noticed. She should have been a dancer, I thought. She laughed as light as a breeze.

Later that night, after a spaghetti and meatball dinner that Kev turned into the civilized world's biggest mess—"They're not softballs, stupid," Geoff had declared, glaring; "No dessert," Mom said, "if you can't keep the meatball on your plate"—the house grew strangely still. All of us in our own places, with our own thoughts, even Kev somewhere off the trouble radar.

I was taking a look at one of Geoff's old SAT books, trying to pack in more vocab for one more round of show-me-you're-smart testing, even though I knew that chances were I had all the words I'd ever learn already stuck up in my head. There's just a certain amount that fits up there, in the landscape of my brain cells. Only a certain number of neurons that work; I was already packed to capacity. I was on my back with the book held above me. I was on my side, then, practically asleep. I was drifting off remembering Mrs. Marksmen with her perfect hand surf when I realized that there was someone at my door.

"Your father has something for you," my mom said when I turned and saw her there. She'd changed into her pajamas—old alma mater sweats from the U of Penn, a worn-out gray T-shirt; and behind her, now beside her, was Dad, blocking the light from the hallway. He pushed himself through the door frame, and they both walked to my bed. Mom sat down, then he did, and then I slid slightly north. I tossed the old SAT book to the floor, where it fell with a thud.

"I didn't bother to wrap it," Dad said, handing me a box. "It's a digital. Small but mighty."

"You got me a camera?" I raised my voice though I hadn't meant to, took the box in my hand, pulled the camera from the wrapping. I'd always envied my ultra-megapixeled-camera-endowed friends. I'd always thought that taking pictures—real pictures—was another way of writing poems. Or reading the poems back later. Or something. Whatever it was, the two were tangled in my mind, and now I heard Kev down the hall, jumping off his bed and opening his door. Kev, a flash of lightning through the dark hall of the house.

"Extra batteries and memory sticks," Dad was saying, and Kev was still running. Down the hall, through my door, a slam against my bed.

"What'd you get her?" he demanded.

"A camera," Mom said.

"How come she gets a camera?" He reached, but I held my camera high. Mom caught Kev's hand gently, tried to nest it inside hers.

"Because she's going to Mexico," Mom said. "Going to see it for the rest of us."

"Mexico is hot," Kev declared.

"Thanks for the info," I said. I lowered the camera, stared through its eye. Turned it on and let it focus. Snapped a picture of my dad.

“So you’re taking pictures for prosperity?” Kev said.

“For posterity,” I said. Dad laughed. Now I turned the camera on Mom and Kev. She’s smiling in that photograph. Kev’s looking half surprised.

nine

The next day I woke to the quadruple clopping of hooves, the slamming and latching of a pickup truck. Boots on asphalt. I grabbed my glasses, sat up. From my bedroom window I could see them best—the long line of trailers that had arrived overnight: from California, Connecticut, New Jersey, from every state that claimed a horse with the heart or brawn to win. The trailers were nose to rear up and down my street—some of them posh as limousines, some with room to spare for the polished carriages and sulkies that would be paraded later that week at the fairgrounds two blocks north.

The horses were like kindergartners being let out of school—shuddering and tossing their tails as they reverse-walked down the grated ramps. Their eyes were as big as purple summer plums, and all I wanted to do right then was breathe in the horses, press my cheek against their cheeks. It was early, a Sunday; I called Riley nonetheless. The horse show came to town only once each year, in May; and the show was a Georgia-Riley tradition.

"Riley," I whispered, so that my brothers couldn't hear. "They've come."

"Who has?" Riley had sleep all over her voice, cob-webs thrown over her vowels. The only thing she knew right then was that I was the one who had called. I'd have felt guilty, except that I didn't. I knew how mad she would have been if I'd let her sleep through any segment of the news.

"The horses."

"Oh my God," she said, her *God* cracking. "Isn't it . . . early?"

"They came in overnight."

"The big ones?"

"Yeah."

"The Falabella, too?"

"I'm looking at it right now, Riley. Still as small as last year, maybe smaller." As I talked, I watched the scene beyond my bedroom window—the little horses mixed up with the big ones, the trainer in the dirty jodhpurs whose chestnut mare was trimming the edge of the lawn across the street. There was some kind of commotion involving a trailer that paralleled my lawn. Two men, maybe three, trying to coax a big horse out from the trailer it had come in so that it could walk down the street and take its place inside a fairgrounds stall. They were calling its name. They were getting nowhere. All the horse would do was whinny. Finally the trainer had turned to see; and this had stirred up the chestnut mare, whose ears snapped forward as she lifted her head, making ripples up and down her neck, like pleats.

"Georgia?"

"Yeah?"

"What's happening?"

"I was just . . . They were just . . ." I couldn't really explain what I was seeing. "Trying to get a big horse out."

"What kind of horse?"

"I don't know." I left the window and went downstairs and over to the front door so that I could get a better look. I stepped onto the porch in bare feet, the cell phone still pressed against my ear. It was as if the volume had been turned way up, as if I'd gone from watching a movie to watching a movie getting made. I could hear the men calling the big horse Don Juan, could hear the horse's hooves striking the truck. Finally the trainer with the chestnut mare gave her reins to another man and walked over Don Juan's way. She sang his name, two syllables. She talked to him so quietly, saying words I couldn't hear.

"What's happening now?" Riley pressed.

"Still unloading Don Juan," I said, then said nothing, because finally the big horse made his appearance—this great white Andalusian, his tail so loose and long that it dragged against the grate and tore itself off and snaked in long white strands toward my lawn. I was wishing, really wishing, that Riley was right there, to share the scene. Near the bottom of the ramp, the big horse skidded, then caught his balance. He stood up proud, and mad.

"You're doing a lousy blow-by-blow," Riley said.

"Well, then get over here."

The trailers had been emptied of their horses by the time Riley arrived; they'd been driven around to the Acme, where they would sit all week on the fringe of the parking lot until they moved off to another town's show. Riley had swept her hair into a barrette, and the cut of her top made her arms seem so narrow. Her mom had dropped her at my curb. It wasn't as if she and my mom ever stopped to talk, ever colluded over their girls.

Now we were out on the street, heading north, climbing the slight incline of the hill. Down below us, a block away, were the fairgrounds. We stopped to get the bird's-eye view. There were the milky blue walls that fortressed in the fair; and there were the flags, as bright as jockey silks, snagging the breeze. To the right were the stables, to the left the exercise rings, and straight ahead, deep in, the shops and vendor stands, the giant Ferris wheel, the alley of games where Riley always won, the fish in the bowls swimming nowhere, sleeping never. Hours from now there would be rich women in ridiculous hats and kids holding cotton candy as high as the Olympic torches. There would be men not smoking their expensive cigars. But at that moment it was only the horses, and the gates were open, and Riley said, "Come on," and we went flying, the two of us, Riley so light on her feet that the only feet to be heard were mine, going down hard on the macadam.

At the fairgrounds, the stalls were one after the other on either side of a dark corridor that was so long, it seemed to bend and then disappear behind horse steam. The floor was hay and the trainers were busy and the long faces of the horses were practically floating over the wide doors of their slatted stalls. It was like being in church, like joining in the hymn—the sawdust and manure, the sound of horse teeth on carrots and sugar. No one minded Riley or me, and we minded no one either, just walked down the corridor between the horses as if we belonged, stopping when we wanted to—to touch the snip or the star on a horse nose. Outside, there were blackbirds overhead on the electrical wires, and the dogs that came to the show every year had begun to chase one another, dig for old bones.

Riley and I had been going together to the show

every year since we were ten, when our parents finally relented and let us navigate the harmless fairgrounds alone. Mrs. Marksmen would drop Riley off at my place, and then Riley and I would walk down the street, me toting my mother's radio-sized cell phone for just-in-case scenarios. When we were younger, Riley would wear big sunglasses and floppy hats, skinny halters, denim miniskirts. Her thighs were always the width of her calves, or almost. She'd throw her sinewy arms around the horses' necks—the ones we were allowed to touch inside the shadows of the stables.

Riley was different at the horse show, always. More introspective, more telling. She spoke to the horses as if they could understand her; and most of the time I think they did, letting her settle her hand on the soft slopes of their noses. "Hello, my love, did you miss me?" she'd say. It seemed they had, that they remembered her year to year, the stories she would tell: small, quiet, whispered stories—revelations, I thought them, disclosures. She'd remove her shades. Toss her hat to the sawdust floor.

"My mother named me Audrey," she had confessed to a gray spotted mare one day, standing on her toes—maybe we were fourteen. "When I was five I started calling myself Riley." The mare had lifted her long nose and dropped it again, grunted politely; Riley continued. "I pretended not to know who Audrey was. It drove my mother crazy, until one day she just gave in; and now probably she doesn't even remember that she named me for the movie star I refuse to be." She'd smiled. She was so pretty when she did.

I'd met Riley the year she'd renamed herself, in kindergarten, a delicate blonde whom we all called Glitter after she started glue-sticking sparkle dust to every single thing—jump rope handles and umbrella stands, easels and paintbrush handles, dollhouses and doll cheeks, the big plastic boxes where the millions of crayons were stored. For the first whole year that I knew Riley, she had sparkle somewhere in her hair or clothes; and always her mother would make a big stink of it, marching Riley over to the sink at the end of each day before she'd drive her home.

"I invented my name," Riley had told that mare. "It suits me." She'd never said where she'd first come upon the name. She always claimed that it was her creation, her first work of art, the first manifestation of her talent.

Once, last year, Riley had gotten obsessed with a chestnut Hanoverian whose name (they hung the horses' names on cards outside each stall) was Windfall. "Oh, you poor thing," Riley had said, looping her arms about his neck. "Windfall is no name for a horse." The horse pricked his ears at the sound of his name, and now he was all Riley's, a captive—Riley, who hadn't said much to me when her mother had dropped her off that day, who had seemed moody, distracted, even testy. I'd tried to get her to talk, but here's the thing: You can't ask Riley a question straight on. You have to wait until she's ready. I'm Riley's best friend because I've always had patience. Because I understand the place where secrets live, and how dangerous it seems to out them.

"Guess," she had said, looking into one of the horse's big eyes, "what happened to me today." Windfall had stirred the straw at his feet with one of his hooves; reading that as encouragement, Riley continued. She spoke so softly that I had to move closer to hear her.

"Well," Riley said. "Well. Some background: My mother is the kind of woman who had a child just because that was the fashion—because there were toddler clubs and play date clubs that she decided to want access into." She pulled a bag of baby carrots from her red cotton tote and put some on her palm and continued talking. Lowering his head, Windfall started chomping. "You need a kid," Riley explained, "to get into kid clubs.

"Well, today, Mr. Windfall, my mother took the cake. At school, like, around noon, we lost all power. Weird, but true. Blue-sky day, no storm coming up, no wind—yeah, I know, I didn't get it either—and still the whole place fizzes. Classrooms go gray. Cafeteria goes cold. The machines in the admin office go quiet. Like dead, you know? A dead zone. We all hung and waited for twenty minutes or so—some teachers still teaching, the cafeteria aides handing out soft pretzels for free because the registers weren't working, the secretaries sitting around on their green metal chairs talking—and then we get word that school is canceled. The buses rolled up, the walkers walked home; but see, Windfall? I don't take a bus and I live five miles away. I've been driven to school since I started going to school—one of my mother's ten commandments. She says buses are just mobile trouble; and besides, driving me looks really good on her mom résumé. She's sensitive, let's put it that way, to people's opinions.

"So I call my mother—you know, the fashion maven, Mrs. Marksmen—with my cell; and she says that it's just *slightly* inconvenient *at this very moment* to stop everything and pick me up, but that she'll get there, she will, give her some time. She says I should stand by the flagpole, where I always wait, and that she'll come when she comes; I should do some homework or something, I should read, stay occupied. So what are my choices, Windfall? What would you do? My best friend over here, she's already on a big bus, headed home."

"Ri . . . ," I started, but she held up her free hand like a traffic cop's stop, and I knew that if I pressed, she'd end her story.

"So, guess what, Windfall," Riley continued. "I sit there, and I'm sketching. I sit there, and I'm reading. I sit there, and above my head the flag is flapping. I sit there, and my butt is hurting from the concrete wall on which I'm sitting. And all this time, my mother never comes. She up and forgets—forgets. It's not like she's got fifty kids to tend to. Somebody called, and after that somebody else, then someone stopped by, and she's feeling sorry for herself because my father's away on another trip, and she's telling that story, and whatever. Whatever Mrs. Marksmen does all day, that's what she was doing while I waited."

"You should have called *me*, Ri," I said, couldn't help myself from again interrupting, from asking, "Why didn't you call me?"

Ri put up her hand again, silencing me with her eyes. "I know my friend's mom would have given me a ride," she continued, keeping her voice low and calm. "I know that. Because my friend is the coolest ever, and so is her mom, and they are always there for me, they always have been—on my gravestone, it's going to read AUDREY (RILEY) MARKSMEN: RAISED BY GEORGIA AND HER MOTHER. But that's not the point. Because the longer I sat waiting by the flagpole watching the teachers leave and the parking lot empty, watching the principal go, even the principal, Windfall—all this time I sat until it was just me and the landscape guys and the security guard—the more I wanted Mrs. Marksmen to feel the shame of having abandoned me for, like, forever. I wanted her to pull up and see that the whole place, practically, was empty, that of all the parents of all the kids in that whole school, she had managed to do the very worst job." Riley's voice was so steady, so quiet, not threatening. Windfall continued to munch from her palm.

"I walked home," she told the Hanoverian. "That's the end of my story. I walked all that way after more than an hour had gone by, in my flip-flops, too, which was, like, a hundred minutes of pure torture. When I opened the door to my house, I found my mother with her knees tucked up to her chin on the white plush couch in the great room, having a cup of ginger tea with Julie Caruthers from down the street. You should have seen the expression on her ravishing face, Windfall. Not concern, it wasn't that. It was embarrassment. 'Nice one, Mrs. Marksmen' is what I said. That's it. Sum total of my accusation and complaint; I'd practiced the sentence all the way home. Mrs. Caruthers left about five seconds later. My mother took me to Georgia's in a snap-of-the-fingers instant."

"Jesus, Ri." I felt sick to my stomach. Clammy. Wrong.

"I didn't say a single word the whole drive over." Ri looked at me then. "For once I didn't have to."

Windfall whinnied to register his opinion. A trainer walked by. We moved on.

This particular day at the horse show, in this summer of Juárez, I'd been telling Riley a story about Geoff. About how he'd come into my room the night before and just hung out until—lightning bolt—I realized he actually wanted to talk. To me. I had grown so used to Geoff's absences, his barricades, his sending Kev away, that I'd stopped hoping for time with him myself.

Because the fact of the matter is that Geoff's an über-talented, funny-when-you-catch-him-right guy, and when he leaves for S. I. Newhouse in the fall, Rennert High will be less than it was. Geoff has been the voice of the school's morning announcements for three years running. He masterminded these insanely popular TV Studio shows. He started a club to help a friend with cancer. Geoff was a million things to a million people—outside in the world, away from home, where I'd concluded he belonged. All through high school I'd been asked one question: Are you really Geoff Walker's sister? And the answer was yes, and I bet you can't believe it, and no, I rarely see him, and when he's home, he's closed his door.

Geoff wore his thick, black hair buzzed close. He wore T-shirts winter, spring, summer, fall, and rotating pairs of jeans. The only variable was his shoes; that night he wasn't wearing any. He just came in, sat at my desk. I put down the book that I'd been reading—Jack Gilbert's *The Great Fires*, which is, I have to say, a really great collection of poems, even if it did come by way of Mr. Buzzby.

"Hey," he said.

"Hey." I put the book facedown on my bed, propped myself up on my elbows. I must have given Geoff a funny look, because he shook his head, said, "What?" in his morning-announcements voice.

"*What* what?" I said. "You're the one who just barged in here."

"Yeah," he said. "Trespassing. I pulled a Kev."

I laughed. "What's up?"

"Miss Barham," he said, "is a *très* cool English teacher. I told her you were going to Juárez."

"You did? You were talking to her about me?"

"It happens." He smiled. "Sometimes."

"Okay." I grew self-conscious; I don't really know

why. Geoff's just my brother, after all.

"Miss Barham suggested Cormac McCarthy," Geoff continued. "You know, as an author to read in prep for Juárez. I was in the library anyway. It was right there; I grabbed it. You know. What the heck." He lifted the book so that I could see the cover. *Cities of the Plain*. A dusty landscape red with fire.

I hadn't noticed until then that he'd had something in his hand, and if I had, I wouldn't have dreamed it was for me. "Wow," I said, flabbergasted. "Well. Thanks."

"No problem, G." Geoff stood, left the book on my desk. He began to cut across the room, then stopped. "Take it easy," he said. "In Juárez, I mean."

"I've got to survive another two months before I'm even on the plane," I said. "Still plenty of time to save you from Kev."

"Yeah," he said, leaving. "What about *that*? Leaving me to the wolves. Thanks a zillion."

This was the story I was telling Ri—the my older-brother-pays-a-visit story—as we stood in the stables among the horses that day. I was going to tell her, too, about some of the research I had been doing, an article

I'd just read: *Across the border from El Paso, Texas, and 15 minutes northwest from Ciudad Juarez, sits a population of people with hopes for a better life.* I was going to say that every time I read about our destination, there were fuzzy collisions of optimism and despair, opportunity and danger, welcome and barbed fences. The ghosts of murdered women. The faces of children left behind. The chance to help. The possibility of being helpless.

But Riley seemed distracted, far away, and finally I stopped, let silence come up between us. I gave her the room I knew she needed if she was going to confide in me at all. I *hoped* she would confide in me. I'd been waiting for it.

"Georgia?" she finally said, her hand on the spotted nose of a pinto whose name, we'd read, was Splash.

"Yeah?"

"I kind of screwed up this year. Academically, I mean." Which I knew, even though we weren't in any of the same classes. School for Riley had always been about her clay pots, her sculptures, her paintings. Her work was hung in the halls on Parents' Night; in the case near the TV Studio they displayed her jewelry; she won scholarships to art camp. Science, math, English, world cultures, foreign languages, were all secondary to Riley. Her intelligence lived in her art. In junior year, especially, her grades had gone south; and every time I'd mentioned the tutoring center or a mentor Geoff himself once raved about, she shut me out. But now it was May, the end of the year. In the fall we'd be filling out our college applications.

"Nothing's permanent," I told her. "You still can fix things."

"I've got a 2.9, Georgia. What college is going to look at me with that? Coming from Rennert High, especially, where a 3.5 is muck."

"You're an artist, Riley. It's your portfolio that counts." I said it because I believed it, and because, within the stable shadows, she looked infinitesimally small. I put my arms around her. "You'll be fine," I told her. "You'll see."

It was right then that we heard the commotion outside, when both of us turned and started hurrying for the door. When we reached that place where the shadows were intersected by the sun, we turned left and looked. There in the nearest exercise ring was Don Juan, dragging his tail like a long white hem.

"That's him," I said to Riley, and she didn't even ask who. She started walking, faster and faster now, toward the big white horse and his trainer and the ring that was full of nothing but them.

"Lord," she said, her voice hushed. "He's gorgeous."

"I told you."

"I mean, really gorgeous, Georgia."

"I know it."

Now she was up against the fence of the exercise ring, braiding herself into its horizontal slats, her body like twine, folding in places mine never would. The trainer glanced our way but didn't mind us. Don Juan stomped and snorted, stepped, studied us. He seemed strong enough and proud enough to save the entire world.

"Mister Don Juan," Riley was saying. "There you go, big guy." He raised his tail and he swung it from side to side while Riley kept talking to him, saying, "You look so fine."

I was watching Riley; she was mesmerized. I shifted my gaze to Don Juan. When I turned to look at Riley again, I saw that she was crying. Big tears, like long rain on bright window. Big tears, drowning out her freckles.

"Hey," I said, and I reached out to touch her—to

put my hand on the small, hard wing of her shoulder. To touch her too-diminished self. "What is it, Riley? What's wrong?"

"He's so beautiful?" She shuddered.

"Yeah?"

"So beautiful, Georgia, and he isn't even trying."

"I get that, Riley. But how's that sad?" *Tell me why you're sad,* I wanted to say. *Tell me why you aren't eating, because I know you're not eating. Look at you, Riley. What's up?*

"If you lived with my mother, you'd know."

"Riley," I said, but she wouldn't say more. *Riley,* I wanted to say, *I'm your best friend. Talk to me, Riley. We can fix this.* But she'd said what she could and there would be nothing else—no more sign of anything wrong until we were too far from home. No more chances that I found or made to get to the heart of our troubles.

PART *Two*

one

We were out of our minds with the heat the second we stepped off the plane. Even inside the El Paso airport we were feeling flattened and woozy as we stood waiting for our bags to spit down the chute and wind their way to us. Mack, Mr. Thom, and Mrs. K. had gone to get the vans that would take us through the heat, across the border, to the church where we'd be sleeping. I'd had to buy a new sleeping bag. I was hoping not to use it.

We stood in the blaze of the sun for an hour—no one even close to straying. Corey and Sam played some kind of card game. Jazzy blew bubbles through huge wads of gum. The guy who didn't talk just stood, staring out toward streets that appeared to be melting.

"You know Dalí?" I heard Sophie say.

"Dalí?"

"The painter?"

"Sure," Riley answered. Casually, not for an instant betraying that art was what she knew.

"He should be here, painting our picture." Sophie threw back her head and made her whole body go loose and limp. She looked, for a minute, like goo. Riley started laughing, and she could not stop. She tossed her arm across Sophie's shoulder: "It's official," she said. "You're one of us."

"Cool beans," said Sophie.

"Don't even talk about beans," Riley said. "We're going to get our fill of those."

Hope you do, I wanted to say.

I didn't.

It took another hour to get to our quarters—past clanked-up cars; past roadside vendors; past women walking, old men walking, children, crowds of children—hundreds of them. They moved along beside the road with steady determination, or they were carried by their mothers, or they were chasing one another, laughing; and where, I wondered, were they going, what was waiting for them, at the end? I pressed against the window and took photographs—through the dust, through the traffic, child after child.

We arrived at last at a tiny, gated-in church located on a hard-dirt road in a part of Juárez where we were not *ever*—we were three times cautioned—to go walking. Some of us were to sleep in the miniature chapel, some in the kitchen, some in the two tight rooms that had probably been designed for storage, and the rest of us up a flight of stairs that seemed to have been nailed there only seconds before our arrival.

"Up there?" Riley asked. We'd sat together in the van, with Sophie one seat up—beside Sam and Corey, who had stopped playing their card game and had stopped talking, too, taking their cues, it seemed to me, from the big guy. It was Jazzy who had provided running commentary as we drove, until even she couldn't think of words for what we saw. Mr. Thom had driven, with Mrs. K. beside him. He was blond and young looking; he was Corey's dad. Mrs. K. had long, brown wavy hair held back by a broad white band. She looked glamorous with her sunglasses on, and she was an older version of her daughter, Catherine, who had traveled in the other van. Now Mrs. K. stood in the courtyard with her suitcase in one hand, looking around at her lodging options, looking, as I'd been looking, at the scarily rickety stairs.

"I'm making a claim," I said, sounding more confident than I felt. I gathered my things, headed for the stairs, tested the first step with my foot. Riley was right behind me, Sophie second. Mrs. K. wasn't too far behind.

"Catherine wants the kitchen," she said as a way of explaining her decision to room with us. She waited until Riley, Sophie, and I had reached the thin plywood landing outside the second-floor room before she started to make her way up. She hoisted her bag high with both her hands, then realized she needed a way of steadying herself. "Well, this is sweet," she said; "the whole thing's swaying." And just like that, Riley was down the steps helping Mrs. K. with her bag. It was half her height and twice her width, that suitcase. I could see only Riley's head and feet.

"If your mother could see you now," I said.

"Except that she can't," Riley said, and yipped.

Again Sophie started laughing. "Don't get her started," I warned. "Believe me."

The upstairs room had just one puny window. It had five bunk beds that were built of wood, and that was it—no sheets, no pillows, no blankets, no mattresses. There was a red-tile floor and a loose pane of reflective glass on the far wall. "For primping," Riley said. Mrs. K. lifted her heat-dampened hair off the back of her neck and removed her huge sunglasses.

"You know what the worst part is?" Mrs K. asked, wiping a bead of sweat off her face.

"What's that?" I asked when it was clear that she wasn't about to answer her own question.

"The worst part is that this was my idea. 'College résumé,' I kept saying. I had to force Catherine to go." I remembered Catherine sitting all sullen faced at the airport and on the plane. I remembered her shoving her way into the van she knew her mother wouldn't be taking.

"I think there's just so much to love," Riley said, and now she opened the plank door that had slammed shut behind us and swung her arms open to Juárez. We stepped out with her onto the wobbly second-floor landing and stood together watching the others below us, watching Sam, Corey, and Jazzy, mostly, who were already deep in a game of Hacky Sack. Corey was going knee-to-ankle with the thing. Then he tossed it off to Sam, who chested it to Jazzy, who meant to hit it with her head, I guess, but it flew past her, hit the ground, threw up a cone of dust.

"My bad," she said.

"Nice," Jon said. He was standing there watching, leaning against the chapel wall beside Mariselle and Neil. They looked odd together, the three of them—Mariselle so tall and Jon so broad shouldered and Neil real skinny—and they had their arms tied across their chests, as if they couldn't decide if Hacky Sack was cool or not, something they should move in on or something to despise.

Finally it was Neil who broke free from the wall. "Yo," he said; and Jazzy tossed him the sack and he spun on one foot, then tossed the thing off his head like Jazzy was supposed to have done in the first place. Sam made a dive for it and saved it, brushed himself off. Corey got it next. He put on a show, then tossed it high; Neil was the one who took over.

"Anyone have a basketball?" Jon asked from the sideline. Nobody answered.

"God, it's hot," Mariselle said. She drew in a deep breath and exhaled, then slumped against the chapel wall as if she were bored already with everything Juárez. Now something caught her eye, and I followed her gaze—straight up to the rooftop next door. There were six men up there, in folding plastic chairs. Maybe I'd have stared, but Mrs. K. was drawing our attention across the courtyard and past the gate toward a little pink stucco house and a slender goose that stood like a guard dog at a post. Beside the goose sat an elderly woman who'd tethered the goose to the stoop with a rope.

"Georgia." Riley nudged me. "Look at that." Outside the gate stood a little girl—dark haired and well dressed and no more than five years old. She was sticking her nose through to our side of things, toward the big guy, Drake the Third, who, I realized, had been nowhere during Hacky Sack. He was kneeling down, making himself her height. He was talking quietly to her.

"Wonder who she is," Riley said.

"Wonder who he is," I said. "I mean, who he *really* is." I took off my glasses, rubbed the lenses clean on my shirt.

Two women in white cooked for us that night—beans that softened to a purple, chicken in a tomato stew, tortillas. There were sodas without ice and sterilized water from a five-gallon jug and some kind of pineapple-watermelon drink that Mack said was safe but that Riley and Sophie and Jazzy and I decided to forgo—all of us sitting together at the two picnic tables that had been dragged out from somewhere onto the rubble. We'd cleaned up a little since the plane and the van, but we still didn't look like much. Sophie's weather-saturated hair fell limply to her shoulders. Riley's streak of orange looked strangely harsh by the light of the setting sun.

Sam and Corey had already made some pact with Neil. Catherine was where her mother wasn't. Jazzy had asked us, "Do you mind?" and Mariselle had come along sighing and stayed—sitting at the table's end, near Mrs. K. The men on the neighboring rooftops had doubled in numbers but were perfectly quiet, peaceful, neighborly even, just catching a breeze on the roof. The goose across the street was still. There was a yellow German shepherd-sized dog whose name was Lobo and who walked around us, nice enough, except for the fleas in his fur and the look in his eyes; and this is what we talked about, the six of us at our crooked table, while the sky turned from blue to black. When Mrs. K. said Lobo might have started life as a wolf, Mariselle rolled her eyes.

"This is a dog that wouldn't hurt one of the fleas on its own back," she declared. She squinted until her eyes got as small as two black dots.

"Do you think it ever rains?" Mrs. K. asked. "In Mexico?"

Now Mack—who hadn't, I'd noticed, been eating at either of the tables—came out of the kitchen and stood by that door. He raised one hand and we all got quiet. "Welcome to Juárez," he said. "We are grateful to Manuel and his family for sharing this home with us, and to Leonor and Concha, who will be keeping you well fed. By now you've all met Lobo." The ears on the old shepherd went up in the direction of his name. He trotted over to where Mack was standing and accepted Mack's hand on his head.

"Today was a long day," Mack continued. "Tomorrow will be longer. Sleep will be the most important thing that you will do tonight. Ten o'clock, lights out. You've got another hour. Remember that we're here as emissaries, as good neighbors. No loud games or noises. No leaving the premises. No flushing anything but the obvious down the toilets. You'll need to be dressed by six tomorrow morning. There'll be cereal in the kitchen."

He bent now to a cardboard box that was by his feet and pulled out a water bottle. "There is one of these for each of you," he said. He reached into his shirt pocket. "And here's a marker. Take a bottle, write your name on it. Take it with you everywhere. Refill it with the filtered cooler water that I provide." Mr. Thom cupped his chin in his hand. Lobo stirred and walked away. Mack said, "I believe Leonor has your dessert prepared," and he stepped aside to let the cook appear with a heaped-high plate of melons. She walked her plate to Mr. Thom's table. Concha followed with a plate for us.

"They must be sisters," Sophie said. "Same size, same eyes, same nose."

"Probably Manuel's sisters," Riley said.

Mariselle yawned to prove she couldn't care less.

"I'm going to take a shower," Mrs. K. announced. "If you girls don't mind." We all understood what she was saying, which was "Please. I'd like to be alone." Even Mariselle nodded; and Mrs. K. rose, made her way up the rattling stairs. Then she came back down with a bundle in her arms and went off toward the bathroom, pulling the plastic curtain door as closed as plastic curtains close.

Afterward—after Mrs. K. was through with her shower and the rest of us had gone two by two into the bathrooms, had brushed our teeth with the water from the cooler, had splashed our faces with the same stuff, had not forgotten (no one did) about the toilet trash—we were upstairs in the dark. I made Riley take the top bunk of our claimed set, afraid that if I did I'd smash straight through. I was the largest girl on this trip to Juárez, and I didn't trust the thin plank beneath me, which made bizarre, creaking sounds when I turned.

"Hey, Riley," I whispered when she was settled in. She dropped her hand over the side. I reached for it. "Sweet dreams," I said. "Okay?"

"Okay." Her voice was quiet. She seemed far away, all the way up there, and I felt all alone in this place to which we'd come—each of us for our own, still-secret reasons. Even the beads on the bracelet Riley had given me didn't glimmer; there was no light shining through the puny window.

Sleep didn't come, not that night. I tried every trick, but I was restless—dreaming when I wasn't even asleep, drifting all around in my mind to thoughts of Kev and my mom, thoughts of the men on the roof, thoughts of the goose across the street, thoughts of Riley above, who was so quiet, too quiet, even in sleep. Who was too thin. I thought of how last night my mom had come to see if I'd remembered what I'd need, then drew me close for a kiss. "You're my daughter," she said, "and don't you forget that."

I said, "Mom, you know I won't."

"Apply your intelligence to every living thing—to where you go, to how you behave, to the way that you look after Riley, because, Georgia, you will have to look after Riley. She's not as good as you are at looking after herself."

"I know that, too."

"Don't drink any water that isn't bottled."

"Wasn't planning on it."

"Don't go anywhere alone."

"It's a cardinal rule."

"Don't think that you have to do everything that the boys do, only better. I know how you are, Georgia. But you leave those saws to them."

I nodded, but it isn't like a nod is a real promise.

Later that night I woke up sweating from a dream, those black wings inside my rib cage beating, my mother's words—*Apply your intelligence to every living thing*—snaking through my blood. Because again my heart knew what my mind had avoided: Juárez was probably a hare-brained scheme; what were the chances—really—that I'd fly all the way there and come home stronger? I fought with the dark to free myself from my bed, struggled to wrest the weight from my chest. It was after two, and the house was quiet, and I headed for the stairs, my right fist against my heart to quiet the fury, to survive it. I needed the night beyond, which finally I reached, stumbling out onto the porch and into the streets and heading for the fairgrounds, which were empty now, the horses long since talked back into their trailers and driven off, Riley's stories floating somewhere in the caverns of their heads. I hadn't had a panic attack in two months. Each one was bigger than the last.

We find out the heart only by dismantling what
the heart knows.

The words are from a poem Jack Gilbert wrote and Mr. Buzzby read toward the end of my sophomore year, when I finally stopped minding the class so much and settled in to learn. I walked the streets that night with that line in my head—walked until I could breathe again and stand up straight without collapsing. I was going to Juárez because I needed some perspective, some place where I could let the big bird free. My head knew things that my heart didn't yet. I was privileged. I was smart. I had a future. It was time to believe in myself.

Now Dad's laugh seemed a million miles away, and Kev didn't seem, in memory, quite so annoying, and I wondered whether Geoff was out or barricaded behind his door. I thought about how cool the air in my own bedroom was. I thought about waking Riley, or even waking Mrs. K., who was breathing hard against her dream, or saying something loud enough for Sophie to hear—Sophie, who was rustling in her own sheets, who was either awake or unwittingly restless; but what would I say if I called to Sophie? Where does a story like mine begin?

I pulled the thin sheet off my legs and crawled out of the hard-plank bed, through the darkest dark. I felt around for the doorknob and opened the door, and then I was outside, sitting on the loose plank landing of the stairs, my knees up under my chin. There was no light to read by, no place to pace, nowhere else to be, no need to put on my glasses. Through the dark I could see the rooftop men who had fallen to sleep in their spectator chairs. Beyond them was the rise of mountains. I heard no morning birds, no honking goose, no Lobo. The day would come. It had to.

I don't know how much time passed. I don't

remember falling asleep, or thinking I would. But when I woke my chin was heavy on the platter of my knees; my mind was chasing some fuzzy tail of a dream. The black night sky was riddled pink. There was the smell of heated butter rising from the kitchen down below. When I turned, I saw Riley in the spot of morning light beside me—so transparent I could almost see through to her bones. Only her hair, which was loose, had some jive to it. The rest of her was like a hologram; I could almost tell myself that she wasn't even there.

"Hey," she said when she felt my eyes on her.

"I thought *I* was supposed to be the insomniac," I told her.

"You can't have it all, Georgia," she said, laughing softly. Her gaze shifted toward the rooftop men—the six of them still fast asleep, their straw hats pulled down on their heads. One had on the most gigantic belt buckle I'd ever seen; it caught the daybreak light and emitted a beam.

"What are you doing out here?" I asked her finally.

"I thought I'd count," she said.

"Count?"

"You know." She reached into the pouch that, I only noticed then, she'd brought to the balcony with her. She opened her hand and held her palm up flat.

"The bracelets," I said.

"Yeah." She placed the one she'd drawn out across her bony lap and reached into her pouch for more. "I hope I have enough."

In the still-new morning light it was hard to make out the colors. There were double rows and triple rows of sparkles, some longer and some shorter, all the beads strung together on wire and clasped like the one I wore. "You're one of a kind, Riley," I said. "Always were and will be."

"Wish I could believe that myself."

"And you've got a real big heart."

She shook her head. "You see those kids along the road today?"

"Of course."

"It made my head hurt, Georgia." By now there were at least three dozen beaded bracelets stippled across her thighs. She reached into her bag and drew out more.

"They seem happy, though. I mean, their faces.

Don't they? Or is it just me hoping, Georgia? I can't figure that out either."

"I don't know."

"Great," she said. "And you're the smart one."

I turned one of her bracelets over in my hand. It was a three-bead-across design, perfectly made. In the morning light it looked like pale blue crystals. It could have been green. It could have been white.

"How are you going to choose?" I asked her.

"What?"

"Choose who gets a Riley bracelet in a country as big as this?"

"That's what woke me up," she said. "Part of my brain was trying to do the math."

"Luck of the draw?" I suggested.

She nodded. "Maybe that's the only way."

"Put them in a sack, line up the children, and let them choose."

"You think Mack will let me take them to the work site?"

"Why not?"

"It's not like I warned him or anything. Not like giving things away is in his book of rules."

"I'll ask him if you want me to."

"Not necessary, but thanks."

The sky around us was brightening. The moon was growing dull. We sat together over another day beginning. The men on the rooftop had started to stir. One tilted his hat in our direction.

"I was afraid of them last night," said Riley, meaning the men. "But that was stupid."

I shrugged.

"Turns out they're kind of nice. Kind of like protection."

"Agreed."

"I keep thinking about my mother," Riley said. "What she'd do if she saw this."

I put my arm across the wire hanger of Riley's shoulders. "I don't know, really. And I don't know if it matters. It's what *you* do that counts. What you see. Who you are."

"I guess so."

Down below, the door to the chapel creaked open. It was Jon, in a towel, making his way to the bathroom. Riley and I didn't say a word. He didn't look up. He never saw us.

"You're always so together, Georgia," Riley said. "You always are."

"Oh, God," I said. "That is just so much bullshit. You should see the inside of my head."

"That'd be something else," she said.

"Yeah. Like a big old biology experiment."

"What's in there?"

"A mess. And you should see my rib cage. I've got a blackbird instead of a heart."

Riley laughed her beautiful laugh.

"I can't do this," Riley said, leaning her head on my shoulder.

"You're here," I told her, and that was all. It was what I'd told myself.

two

A little later we were all packed tight into our rented vans and out in Juárez, on the road. We'd loaded the five-gallon water jugs, and all the tools and clothes we could fit were in the back—the hammers and work aprons and thick cotton gloves we'd all been told to bring from home, along with the more complicated stuff that the guys had pulled from the back of Manuel's chapel. It wasn't even seven A.M., but it was hot, and there was only one music station on the van radio that worked and a single speaker through which the tinny music floated. Jazzy, Sophie, Mariselle, Riley, and I all looked like newbie candy stripers in our second-hand scrubs. Catherine was in the other van, but so was Mrs. K.

I was in the middle of the middle, a really bad spot. Too far back to get any benefit from the timid AC, too squeezed in to make much use of the digital camera on my lap, too sweaty hot to keep my glasses up high on the bridge of my nose. I had Riley on the one side and Mariselle on the other—shoulder to shoulder, thigh to thigh, and sticking-to-each-other hot. Mariselle's sighs were in endless supply. Riley had started sighing in stealth imitation; and Sophie, up in front of us, was perfecting The Mariselle, too, except that Mariselle never noticed—she was far away in her head, thinking her immensely sighable thoughts.

The roads nearest our living compound were dirt finished off with dust; they finally led to asphalt-paved stretches. The stores along the roads sold secondhand hubcaps and steering wheels, used tires, roof tiles, panes of glass; and sometimes there were closet-sized stores that seemed to specialize in plastic toys or laundry detergent or cans of soda stacked in blocks of vaguely yellow cooler ice. There were people walking, people driving, people sitting up on roofs, people in buses, people in shirts and dresses that were vivid, bright, so bold; and I thought about *las muertas de Juárez.* I wondered how anyone could disappear when so many eyes were watching.

The farther we drove, the wilder and more dangerous the driving got, and there were stretches that were probably a dozen lanes across, and stretches where the roads split and then rammed back into one, and a tunnel beside a bridge, and a sudden concrete barrier wall; and then at last the road bent along the river.

"El Paso," Mack said from his driver's seat, and we all turned and looked past the sludging Rio Grande toward a stand of sleek American banks and silver corporate headquarters and comfortable-seeming universities and regular-looking stores with honking-big logos nailed way up high like ads for people who could never buy whatever was being sold. It gave me the strangest feeling to see my country from the other side of the fence. To be among the million in junker cars who would have to pay, somehow, to get out.

"Lord, it's hot," Sophie said, and from the curl of her ponytail hung a suspended bead of sweat. Jazzy, who was sitting beside Sophie, started beating her hand like a fan. Riley started fanning, too, but none of us were better off.

Mack kept driving, with Mr. Thom's van sometimes behind, sometimes beside. The road eventually skinnied down. We reached an intersection, and Mack signaled to go left; and just as he turned, I saw a side-of-the-road man holding high this huge, ugly fish, like another kind of sign. That fish had the fattest lips I'd ever seen. Its scales had a grotesque pinkish tint. The eye I could see reminded me of a bashed-in metal bucket. "I'm never eating sushi again," Jazzy said, but only Riley laughed.

It took us fifty minutes to go fifteen miles; and then the streets deteriorated to thick, hard sand and we were turning left into a *colonia,* Mr. Thom's van still right behind. Now we were the only two vans anywhere for as far as we could see, and the streets were wide, whitish, and, it seemed, vacant; and Mack turned off the radio so the only thing we heard was silence, which was louder than all the noise we had up until then been driving through. Even Mariselle did not sigh.

I leaned forward, lifted my camera. I zoomed in and

out, framed Anapra as I first saw it. Familiarity doesn't do photographs any good. What is news to you is news to the lens, and that's where art comes from; and also when you are looking through a camera's eye, you see things you wouldn't otherwise.

There were mattresses for dividing walls between the broken houses, cacti in tire planters, a mule in a yard, the bruised-looking veins of electrical wires in a sprawl down one bleached hill.

Finally we caught sight of a broom truck up ahead painted fire engine red. The bristles of the brooms poked upward, toward the sky, as if to scrub the air. The driver had his windows down and his radio blaring, and all of a sudden I was thinking about the old neighborhood ice cream truck. About Kev rushing out on summer evenings to get his Fudgsicle.

There was a foulness in the air: the open sewer lines. There was a crowd of wild dogs. There was a doll that had been thrown to the roof of a tar-paper house, like some kind of sacrifice. The dust was earth and air and sun. There were no children anywhere. There were no people we could see; and Riley looked at me, and Sophie looked at Riley, and Jazzy sighed even before

Mariselle did, and Mack said, "Welcome to Anapra."

I took a photograph of that sign. I took photographs of air and sun, of that doll on the roof, of the dogs—and the word for them was *feral.* Then I turned and took a photo of Riley, whose bones were so close beneath the skin of her face, whose eyes were big and hungry.

three

Out in the heat, on the work site, it was just like what we had seen on Mack's aerial drawings: a cluster of three pale blue stucco buildings nested high on a plateau of sand. Anapra lay below the compound. Mountains rose behind—scruffy and mostly bald, except for the occasional clumping of gray-green and yellow weeds; I never got a good photo of those mountains, I never captured that gray-green.

One of the buildings was long and rectangular, with a kitchen on one end and wooden tables and benches everywhere else except at the other end, where a toilet sat behind a door. One was a two-room house with an attached shed. The last was a tiny chapel half the size of my bedroom, with a rose-colored carpet on the floor. There were wooden monkey bars on the plateau, a sandbox with a roof, a swing. The ground was sand so coarse and thick that I felt myself going ankle deep when we walked and when we stood. We were gathered now in a semicircle around Mack. Beside him was a short man whose name, we learned, was Roberto González. Roberto had a wife, Lupe, who stood in a triangle of shadow. She was just as short as the man she'd married, but there were more lines around her face, more places etched by sun.

I had my camera around my neck. I took their photograph.

"Five years ago," Mack was saying, "Roberto and his wife presented their compound to Anapra. They built this playground for the children. They opened the chapel to guests, to meetings, to songs. They converted an old shed into a kitchen and encouraged community meals on Saturdays after mass, and they did this because Anapra is their home, because they understood that God had given them more than many others. Roberto and Lupe have two daughters. Both now live in the States. One is a nanny and one is a maid. They send part of their wages home. It was from the employer of the elder González daughter that we at GoodWorks learned the González story, and of the quest to build a community bathroom."

Roberto stood in the sun while Mack was talking, squinting straight ahead. Lupe maintained her spot in the wedge of shade, wiping her broad hands across her apron, stealing looks at us. There were little rivers of sweat running down my back, a gathering heat around the waistband of my scrubs. Riley had swept her hair high, away from her face.

Mack was explaining now—processes and precedence, expectations and rules, the little things that would, he said, determine our success. He was drawing the basic footprint of the bathroom with his foot, sketching out something long but not so wide that would sit between the house and the kitchen. He was describing the *pipas*—tanker trucks that drive water to the dunes and fill the concrete cubes that store the drinking water. He was saying that we were all so lucky that Mr. Thom wasn't just Corey's dad but an architect, too, and that as builders we'd be taking our instructions from him, working in teams, getting things done. "I don't care who you are or where you've come from," Mack said. "For the next two weeks, building a bathroom is your purpose. Leave Anapra better than it was, and you will have made a difference."

Mack stepped aside so that Mr. Thom could take the center spot in our semicircle and tell us in fuller detail about the days ahead. In the shed of Roberto's house we'd find what we'd need, he said—shovels, ladders, buckets, wheelbarrows, even a circular saw. The two-by-fours and two-by-sixes would be arriving later that day, in the back of a truck. "Thanks, by the way, Drake, to your dad for underwriting the lumber," said Mr. Thom. I glanced at Drake beneath his maroon baseball cap. He didn't so much as blink. I looked again at Mr. Thom, whose short blond hair was white in places and whose eyes were blue and serious now, though once, I imagined, they were full of something else: mischief, maybe, or ambition.

"Our first task," Mr. Thom continued, "is digging. We'll need a foundation for the bathroom's concrete pad. We'll also need the six-by-six-by-eight-foot hole that will be the septic tank. I want the guys on the tank hole. I want the girls for the foundation. I want everyone paired up in teams. Partners, head over and see Roberto. He's got your bucket and shovel. He'll show you where you're tossing the sand."

Mr. Thom stopped talking, and Sophie grabbed Riley before I could. "Thanks a whole lot," I said to Riley with my eyes.

"You want bucket duty or shovel duty?" I asked Catherine as she fitted a baseball cap down on the curl cascade of her head.

"Bucket, I guess," she mumbled.

"Bucket it is." I grabbed the shovel.

We waited then, watched and waited, while Mr. Thom and the other adults except for Lupe drew out lines in the sand. I glanced over at Sophie and Riley, who were standing against the farthest wall in the thinnest strip of shade, laughing at something, Riley shaking her head so that her earrings clattered, all thirteen against one another. I drew my camera to my eye and snapped a photograph. I went around the circle taking photos—portraits for later. So that whatever happened here would be real, wouldn't be erased by time. Could go home with me, to my family.

We broke for lunch shortly before noon—filed into Lupe's kitchen, which had been steaming all morning long with smells of poultry and spice. There were women with Lupe whom I hadn't seen before—two older ones, and one young and pretty. They had lined up vats and trays and jugs of things; there were paper plates and plastic forks. We stood in line and we got served; and though the oven heat had made it hotter in that kitchen than it was outside, there was the shade of the roof, and there was Riley, saving me a seat on a splintering bench. I held my plate high and climbed in beside her. My shirt was sweat-glued to my back.

"Girl shovels a mean bucket of sand," Sophie said, nodding Riley's way.

"You should have seen Georgia," Catherine said, for she had swung her legs in next to mine. We'd gotten along after all, Catherine being the kind of person, I'd discovered, who likes to get things done: a forward in soccer, the president of Big Buddies Club—stuff she'd told me as we worked. "Let's get it over with" is what she'd said at first, out there in the sun; and it didn't matter how many shovelfuls of sand I'd come up with, she could carry the heaping bucket all the way around back and return with it empty in no time.

"Georgia does everything well," Riley said. She puckered up and blew me an air kiss, then threw her skinny arm across my back. I forgave her right then for teaming with Sophie. It wasn't her fault, after all, that she was so completely likable.

"Glad I'm not on septic tank duty," Sophie said, rolling her eyes. "Did you see the size of that hole?"

"Puhl-lease," Riley said, pushing away her plate. "Can we talk about something else at lunchtime?" She hadn't eaten a thing and she was making like she was done—talking about the holes and the heat and the González family and their community bathroom dream. Everyone else was passing their plates for more, and the din around us grew. A big, complicated conversation had begun at our table's end. In that tumult, I leaned in close to Riley.

"Yo," I said. "Lunch. Have some."

"Would rather not." She wrinkled her nose.

"You have to eat something, you nut."

"I had breakfast."

"Yeah, and that was, like, ten days ago."

"Don't worry about it, Georgia."

"Don't worry about it?"

"Yeah. Like, what's it to you, anyway?"

I could have gone with that. I could have paid attention—pulled up, backed off, joked the line away, retreated. I could have acquiesced, let Riley rule like Riley always ruled; but I'd reached the end of my rope with my best friend's charade. I hung suspended, undecided, before I barreled through. Crossed a line that we had, between us and for all of time, honored. From best friendship to something else. In but an instant. Just like that.

Do the right thing, you risk ruin.

Choose responsibility, and don't think that makes you someone's hero.

"Too late, Riley. I *am* worried." I sat close, spoke softly. I touched her toothpick arm with my epic hand, and that was it: She snapped. Leveled me with her sapphire eyes. Snatched her hand away.

"I think you should mind your own business, Georgia," she said, her voice whisper fierce. "Do I watch what *you* eat? Do I tell *you* to cut back? Do I say, 'Hey, you'd be so much cuter if you just didn't eat so much'?"

"I'm not shrinking," I said, glaring back, feeling my face turn red. "I'm not risking my health to disprove a mother's theory. I'm not starving myself so that I won't be average, because you know you're not, Riley. That's stupid. That's you being stupid for listening to her." I was talking under my breath, under the spitting clamor of the crowded room. Riley sat acting violated. Pissed off. Unrelenting.

"You're also not my mother," she warned. "Okay?"

"I know what you're doing, Ri. Jesus, look at yourself. You're like a walking advertisement for anorexia."

Her eyes were a cold burn, stalactite ice. "That's nice, Georgia. That's real nice. I'll try not to forget that you said that. Like, ever."

"Trying to help," I said, lowering my voice to a true whisper, pleading with her now, not just to hear me but to listen. To stop walking away. To come back. *Please, Riley. Come back.*

"News flash, AP Queen. I happen to know what I'm doing. When I want your help, I'll ask for it. And I don't really see that happening. Not in a long time. Not in probably forever."

She threw another look my way—knives in my gut.

Then she smiled, pushed back, stood up, called out to Sophie, said, "I've got something to show you." So that now the two of them were going off somewhere, knotted together like best friends.

Others were clearing plates and forks. I gathered Riley's things with mine, dumped the mess of everything in the trash, and went outside and handed Catherine the shovel. Across the courtyard stood Sophie and Riley, Riley showing off the bracelets that she wore, twisting every last one around on the skinny twig of her arm, as if jewelry were her secret.

"I'll take bucket duty," I told Catherine; and together we walked back to the job, me slipping gracelessly in that sand—me too big, too wide footed, too hurt and angry to navigate anything gracefully.

We worked, silent but effective, all afternoon long. With the heat on our backs, with the sun in our eyes, beneath no rescuing shade, we shoveled and carried, dug out our fraction of the foundation pad. There wasn't time or reason for chatter, no time to seek an apology from Riley. No reason to expect one.

Finally it was time to drive the fifty minutes back to Manuel's compound—back to the crooked stairs and the dog named Lobo and the men on the roof in their chairs. I sat beside Catherine, in a window seat. I took photos of every last thing I saw.

"You an artist now?" Riley asked from the backseat.

I turned and gave her a funny stare. "For prosperity," I said.

She scowled. She met my eyes and stared straight through them. Then she set her jaw and turned.

four

Back at the compound, after dinner, Mack told a story. Dead tired, we sat slumped at our picnic benches—showered and fed but still grimed by sand, the close-to-the-noseness of the sewage. Mack sat in a fold-up chair before us. There hadn't been a cloud all day, and now the sun was falling, a last gasp of orange in the sky. Lobo was sprawled out at Mack's feet, hoping for some leftover salsa guacamole, maybe, or just a touch of a hand, someone to scratch away the fleas.

Riley was sitting with Sophie; I sat as far from them

as I could. My choice. Me snubbing Riley so that she couldn't get her own snubs in.

You can't help people who won't help themselves.

You can't chase vanishing acts.

You can't go around acting as hurt as you feel. People will notice. They'll say things.

"By now you have all formed your first impressions of Anapra," Mack had begun, unknotting a battered bandana and combing his blonded hair back with one hand. He looked tired, full of ache. He wore no ring on any finger, just one gold earring in one lobe. "That makes you one of many in a movement. Some of the pallet houses you see in Anapra have been built by high schoolers from Arizona. Some of the straw bale homes were put there, in part, by a team of American architects. Those Afghan pine and Italian stone pine trees you saw growing were planted with the help of Texans. Just two weeks ago, the church across the way from Roberto's chapel was painted by a team that came from Denver. You are officially part of something bigger than yourselves; and I know you're tired, and I know it's hot, and I know that you're a long way from home. But today was the beginning of two weeks that will transform you. Keep your eyes open, and your hearts."

Lobo yawned, stood, walked a circle, and lay back down. Looking through the square windows of the kitchen, I could see Leonor and Concha working at the sink—one of them washing our dishes, one of them drying, a bare yellow lightbulb hanging above their heads. Leonor wore a checkerboard towel across one shoulder; as she talked, Concha laughed, as if washing dishes were the best part of their day. I thought about home and all my complaining when I had to load the dishwasher, and I stole a look at Riley, whose mother had a rule against doing any kitchen work herself. The sun had burned the mist across her nose. She was charming the hell out of Sophie.

"Now I know, because I hear you talking, that you minded doing battle with the dust," Mack went on. "And I'm not going to sit here and pretend that I like it myself. Anapra was desert before it was a *colonia*. It wasn't a place that people chose to live until the *maquiladoras*—the assembly plants—went up along the border. Good for the economy, maybe. Bad for the environment and for the people who need to find a place to live somewhere close to their employment. The aquifer that

Juárez shares with El Paso is drying up. Tuberculosis and malaria and hepatitis are constants.

"So the dust is bad; it's devastating. But more than that, for people who aren't blessed like you and I have been blessed, it kills. Not long ago in Anapra, a seven-month-old boy choked to death on it. His lungs were thick with the stuff; his house had been open to the wind. He was a baby, and the air killed him. And this is life as thousands know it in Anapra."

I saw Drake close his enormous eyes. I saw Mrs. K. reach to touch Catherine's hand. Jon crossed his arms, and Corey did, then Sam and Neil crossed their arms, too, as if they could protect themselves from the news they'd heard, or from the heartache of Anapra. I wouldn't look at Riley to see how she felt. I didn't need to know.

"It's one thing to come to Juárez and be reminded of your own good fortune," Mack continued. "But the question is: Will that be enough? Is simply knowing that you are better off going to define you?"

He left the question hanging. He stood up, and Lobo stood with him, the dog's nose high and hopeful, as if Mack had some treat stashed in a pocket. Manuel appeared from out of the shadows. The lightbulb had gone off above Leonor and Concha.

"The day is getting on," Mrs. K. said.

We sat there, still. Riley had turned and was looking my way—one quick, small glance. Hurt eyes. I shrugged. Made like I didn't care.

In *Cities of the Plain*, McCarthy's book, John Grady is a cowboy who loves whatever he finds so much that he makes it his business to protect it. He loves the horses on the ranch where he works with his best friend, Billy. He loves the pup whose brother dies, loves the epileptic prostitute whom he finds in a whorehouse in Juárez. He takes the whole throb of life upon his shoulders, and he's a hero, but he's also doomed—you can just feel it; you know he's not going to survive the excess of his self-inflicted caring. You grow up being told that *responsibility* is a good word, that you should step forward first, that you should manage. But the truth is: Too much responsibility gets you into trouble. It boxes you in, divides you into two very different, separate people. Your responsible, solid version is what everybody comments on: *Georgia's reliable. Georgia will do*

it. Georgia always knows what she is doing. She will come through. Your private, hidden self, meanwhile, would shout a different story.

That night, after Mack's talk, I told myself that I didn't need Riley, that I could do without her, that she was wrong, dead wrong, and apologizing was her business. That I'd wait for her to come to me—wait her out, ignore her so bad that in the end she could no longer afford to ignore me. I sat alone as if I didn't mind the alone. Studied the photos I'd taken that day—spinning them backward and forward on that little, glassy screen. Riley before the fight. Anapra afterward. Before and after. After and before. The sun went down to a certain place and then held off sinking farther. The next time I looked up, I saw that dark-haired girl. Standing at the gate alone, peering in and up.

She had on a different dress—a sun-faded yellow that seemed as if it had been worn for years by various sisters, neighbors, strangers. Lobo trotted to her first. Manuel called out to her and waved. Somebody had taken care with the young girl's hair, fixing it with bows. She wasn't wearing any shoes. I lifted the camera and zoomed the lens. She was missing her front teeth.

We were to go nowhere by ourselves in Juárez, yet here was a child out alone at dusk. In fifteen minutes the sun would drop, and the goose across the street was still, and the old woman had left her post—must have been asleep already inside her house that could not have been more than the length of her short body wide. The men on the neighboring roof had settled into their spectator chairs, and over at another table, a game of travel chess was going.

Meanwhile, Riley and Sophie were playing hangman, Riley drawing her stick figures with such high-fashion detail that soon Sophie called Mariselle and Catherine to see, and soon it wasn't even hangman anymore but a game in which a style—punk modern, runway chic, debutante ball, grunge—was being blurted out and Riley was asked to draw it. It was as if they couldn't trip her up. Whatever she drew they loved; they called it perfect. They'd struck at the vein of Riley's talent in hardly more than a day—all it had taken was a game of hangman. I'd known Riley almost forever; but here she'd been discovered, and I could see the glow working on her, convincing her of something she couldn't find at home and taking her further and further from her need to talk to me.

Sometimes color is all there is; and as the sun now fell fast, I photographed its dying pink until the moon was higher than the sun and it was shadows I saw through my camera's eye—blues leaning into blacks and blacks spattered through with the violet. The shapes of men on the roof. The bulge of a mountain range beyond. The old cross that rose from the chapel's roof, which was a rusty color.

The men in their folding chairs lit cigarettes. I sat there watching them, watching the last of the daylight fall across the balcony, until that's what I wanted—that balcony, that light. I walked toward the steps and climbed them. They creaked beneath my weight. Then I stood there looking out, taking photos that would never mean a thing. They mattered only in the present tense, gave my solitude a purpose.

It was then, from up there, that I noticed Drake pushing back from the game of chess and walking toward the gate. He had his hand on Lobo's head, and now he was kneeling down, talking to the girl who stood peering in. Taking something from her outstretched hand, turning to admire it, then slipping whatever it was back through the gate. It was as if the girl had known Drake for a long time. As if one can make a friend that quickly, which, it seems, some people can.

"Riley's walking runway," I heard Sophie call.

And then I watched as below me Riley pretended to model the clothes that she'd just drawn.

In the bunk beneath Riley, I couldn't sleep. Couldn't stop hoping, stupidly hoping, that she'd turn and whisper, "Good night, Georgia. Love you." Turn and say she understood, that she'd get help, that she'd stop starving herself, that she was grateful. But the space above my bed was silent. Riley didn't so much as rustle her sheets. I couldn't tell if she was sleeping, couldn't know what she was thinking, couldn't confront her, because this is a fact: Silence defeats like nothing else does. There is no fighting it.

"You an artist now?" she'd sneered. I remembered freshman year, when Riley's watercolors had taken first place at districts. It was a pretty big deal, and Rennert High was throwing a reception in the lobby bordered by admin and the cafeteria. I'd driven with her and her mother, worn a sorry shade of peach—

a dress that I had bought too small, hoping it would fit me. By the time we'd arrived, the lobby was packed and Riley's watercolors were already strung up on movable boards. She'd given crazy titles to each one—random mind bursts, she'd confided to me the day before, when she was telling me what to expect at the show. "The titles just occurred," she said, titles such as "Believe Me I Tell You" and "What Are Mirrors For?". I knew that they meant more than that. I knew, but I didn't insist that she come right out and say it, because that was back then, when I left her boundaries sacred. When I chose friendship over truth.

In the lobby, the art teachers had gathered and the principal, too, and there were kids we ate lunch with, kids from Riley's art class, a couple of Mrs. Marksmen's friends. Somebody started clapping, and then other people did, and soon the crowd divided in regular Red Sea fashion so that Riley could pass through and stand in the space between the principal and her teachers. She was to be commended, it was said. She had set a new art standard.

"Riley Marksmen has graced Rennert High with her talent," the principal declared, and I will never forget the expression on my best friend's face when she looked toward her mom. It was as if none of the rest of us mattered that night, as if none of the rest of us had come. The point for Riley was that Mrs. Marksmen see that her only daughter was growing up to be someone.

What was I going to see of Riley going forward? How much of her would ever let me back in? I lay in that dark, and the sadness grew wings and the wings were a thrashing and the thrashing was my heart. Panic's a bully. It hunkered heavy on my lungs. I sucked in air and I spat out that hot air. I pressed the hand I could lift to my chest.

So what if panic attacks are a body's defense—the afterbirth of the fight-or-flight response that is wired into our brains? So what? Explanations mean squat. Something ignites, adrenaline flows, a body succumbs, I was desperate. Alone in a room of girls, alone and dying. Waiting for the panic to finish with itself. To fly back into the cage from which it had come.

Apply your intelligence to every living thing. That night I couldn't think of anything but this: Riley had been my one best friend since I was five. And now she lay above me. Silent.

Because of something I'd said.

Because of my loving too much.

Because I'd been a coward for way too long, and I'd let it come to this.

five

It was on the second day that the children came. The sun was high, and Mr. Thom had sent four of us to the top of the hill with the hope, he'd said, that we'd report back with some news. Four of us—me, Sophie, Drake, and Riley—randomly chosen, or maybe not so randomly; I couldn't tell. But I had my camera, and I was using it as a shield, even as it let the strange world in. The white avenues of sand. The pallet houses. The doll that was still sacrificed to the sun. A pack of dogs was yipping through the streets, the dogs' shoulders down and their noses to the ground, as if on the hunt for a bone greased with meat. The brain inside my skull was char. Not one of us was talking.

Maybe we'd been watched the day before and branded friendly. Maybe the heat wasn't as harsh as it had been. I can't explain it. But it is true, what I told you before: That day the children came running. I can't tell you who dared first—which door opened, then shut, leaving the house less crowded. What I know is that it was probably the loveliest thing that could have happened to me at the worst time of my life. It was color like sky—pinks, blues, and yellows. Color bright and clean in a desert place. In my camera's eye. In my head.

"This is so *wild*," Sophie said; and Drake just hovered; and Riley said to no one, or maybe to herself, "They might as well be flowers, blown right off their stalks."

Despite the sun and the uptilting slope of the hill, these kids didn't walk. Even the brother who was carrying his baby sister never slowed for a second, his body bent forward at the waist. There were brothers who came with brothers and clusters of girls and those who came from what must have been east by themselves, all of them dressed in parakeet colors; and I remember a pair of shining patent leathers, throwing the sun back up to the sun. I remember taking that photograph. Sun like bleach, like stain.

Riley's sapphire eyes were platters; for one bright instant they turned and took in the me behind my camera—took me in—and I snapped that portrait. The loose hair at the back of Sophie's neck corked, anticipated, seemed ready to flee. Still, it was Drake who went to tell Mack, and Mack who brought Roberto, and Roberto who called out to the children by name, waving them up the hill faster. The first to reach the top of the hill was a pair of brothers with bright blue eyes and red paisley bandanas that tied back their thick, black hair. Some buttons on their shirts were missing. Their pants were light and loose. When they got to where we were, they hung their heads a little bit, but that didn't disguise their smiles.

The others were right on their heels. A boy in a strawberry-colored sleeveless shirt who had lost his front teeth. The girl with the black patent leather shoes. Several children—both boys and girls—wearing the same red paisley as the bandana boys. There were streaming colors in the hair of the girls—crimson bows and silver strings, wide navy blue bands striped with mango—and I kept thinking how much those kids must have been loved, how beautiful they'd been made by their mothers before they'd left their shacks and gone into the streets and trusted us to receive them. I thought that, and I took photographs. Portrait after portrait, and then I again turned the camera to Riley's face as she stood there in the circle of children, as she reached her hands toward them.

Roberto had a hug for every kid. Mack a handshake, a clap on the back. Now any of us who hadn't been on break were on break, clustering around while the kids began to hang themselves from the monkey bars or sit on the roof of the sandbox or go back around to Roberto's shed and return with plastic baseball bats and a seriously deflated soccer ball.

"Look," Riley was urging Sophie, but I was the one who turned to see Drake with a girl sitting high on his shoulders and another kid—couldn't have been more than four—reaching up to hold his hand.

By now Riley had her own little person dangling from her hand—a miniature girl with gaps between her teeth and eyes that weren't brown but copper. The boy with the strawberry-colored shirt was alone. I went to him, and he opened his arms. I stooped to pick him up. *"Hola,"* I said. He pointed to a plastic bat. When I put him down, he dropped to the gravelly dust and with his hands began to shape a pitching mound. He was flocked to by others, and now they were kneeling, too—building up a mound of dust so that a game could start.

Corey grabbed a stick and started drawing out the plates. Sam took first, Jon second; third went to Neil. Behind home plate the kids of Anapra lined up, mostly boys, except for this one girl who was tall and knobby kneed, with hair that had been chopped short. The Third strode out onto the mound. He underarmed a Wiffle ball to the kid in the strawberry-colored shirt.

An hour later we were all crowded into Lupe's kitchen—us, the Anapra kids, some mothers and fathers who had come up the hill with shy smiles on their faces and gold crosses hung at their necks. Some of the littlest kids sat on our knees; some tucked in close beside us; the patent leather–shoe girl had climbed back up to her post on the Third, who held one of her ankles with his hand while he ate so that she wouldn't fall. Every now and then she'd drum on his head, and I guessed that was their sign, because the Third would stop whatever he was doing and hand her a wedge of the watermelon that Lupe had stacked on a plate at every table.

On my own lap was a child who'd climbed up in all the chaos of the lunch hour and stayed put, perhaps sensing protection in my bigness, some kind of well-defended shelter. She had a little bit of green in her very dark eyes, and lots of light in that green. She had her hair in pigtails and a fringe of bangs, and her eyelashes were tangled and dark as daddy longlegs legs—so long that they cast shadows on her cheeks. Her orange tank top had a satin bow at its neck. Her canvas shoes seemed new.

In the room the noise was big and confused; but it was good noise, mostly Spanish or bad attempts at Spanish, and laughter when the words didn't come out right. Noise I could lose my self within. Mack and Roberto stood together at one end of the room, chatting with Lupe, drinking tall glasses of juice, getting down to the business of the dark stew that Lupe had ladled onto our plates a little while before—stew that Jon called rooster casserole just to make Neil laugh, which he did. I tried to keep my eye on Riley, but she kept vanishing from view. I helped the girl on my lap with her fork. She chewed about a million times before she finally swallowed.

"Georgia," I said, pointing to myself. "Georgia."

She understood. "Georgia," she said.

"¿Cómo te llamas?"

"Isabela."

"¿Cuantos años tienes?"

"Cinco."

"Five," I said, putting up my hand and stretching out my fingers.

The child nodded again. *"¡Hola!"* she said.

Now all eyes were on Mack, who had clapped his hands to get our attention. Even the Anapra kids who couldn't understand his English grew quiet—their parents, too—as he explained the work we were to do that afternoon: how some of us would be lining the big, deep hole with concrete block, and others would be mixing and pouring the concrete that would form the foundation of the bathroom proper, and two would be needed to finish the forms into which the concrete pad would be poured. Any way we chose, he said, it was heavy work made even tougher by the sun; and we were not to overwhelm ourselves, not to push so hard that we wouldn't be able to push as hard tomorrow.

"This is not a race," he said. "The key here is pacing. You're going to watch out for yourselves, and you're going to watch out for each other."

He told us to grab a last piece of watermelon, clean up our places, and fill our water bottles. He said, "The sun is high. Go get your sunblock." Then we said, "*¡Gracias!*" to Lupe as we filed out into the heat, the Anapra kids still mixed in with us, the Third still necklaced with the little girl. What we needed had been laid out for us by Roberto and Mack when we'd been playing ball. I chose the mix-the-concrete station after Riley announced that she'd be happiest toting block. "Given the choices," she said, and laughed. Everyone but me laughed with her.

I lined up with Sam, Mariselle, Mrs. K., Corey, Catherine, and Jazzy, who couldn't decide until Mr. Thom pointed her in the direction of our crowd. "I can't even make brownies," she whined as Roberto demonstrated so many parts cement to so many parts gravel to a lesser water part—the dry stuff mounded high like a volcano and the water poured in last, and big shovels used to turn, fold, and mix. You had to be strong to do the stirring; you had to stick with it, find the right grip; and you couldn't think about anyone or anything else when it came your turn to stir.

We shoveled the first batch into a wheelbarrow, and Sam took over from there, his light-colored eyes squeezing in on themselves as he pushed his cargo across the thick, loose sand and tried his best not to sink. Corey sang Sam some song of encouragement, and then the kids of Anapra joined in, singing some other song of their own from wherever they sat—some on the roof of Lupe's kitchen, some on the rungs of the monkey bars, some in the shade, some up high on the cliff that overlooked Roberto's compound. Chins on their knees, they sang, arms linked together; and finally when Sam got the wheelbarrow the whole fifteen-or-something-foot distance, the kids let out a cheer so big that even Sam, his entire blond head wringing sloppy wet with sweat, had enough in him to take a 360-degree bow.

The concrete we'd made filled a fraction of a fraction of the formed-out foundation hole.

"I am predicting," Mrs. K. said, "that we shall be here forever."

Mariselle sighed.

"Think of it as an adventure," Riley called from around the corner. Some people laughed.

six

We didn't get back until five, each of us kids disappearing at once to the bare shelter of our beds while the adults went off to take their showers. I was disgusting hot, a crust of sweat on every inch of skin, my hair mopped down around my face and too stiff with salt even to comb my fingers through.

I must have closed my eyes; I don't remember. All I know is that when I woke up, I was the only one in that upstairs room. I lay in the afternoon shadows, then slid out of the bunk toward the door, stood on that balcony, looked down. There was not an inch of shade on the balcony. In the courtyard, Catherine and her mother were husking corn with Leonor. Sam and Corey were balancing wood shafts on their fingers—scraps of lumber they must have found lying around. Sophie, Mariselle, and Riley sat in battered beach chairs reading the magazines that Mariselle had stowed in her carry-on luggage like some kind of contraband. They could have been girls at a salon letting their pedicures set. Even if I'd not been at war with Riley, I'd have no business there.

I turned back into the room, grabbed my things, reemerged. Halfway down the steps, I heard Drake and Manuel in the chapel doorway talking. Part English. Part Spanish. The subject was Socorro—the girl, I realized, who stood outside the complex gate. Drake was asking questions, pressing.

I stepped into the bathroom, pulled the shower curtain shut. I didn't turn the water on. Socorro's sister was dead, I'd heard Manuel say. She'd been taken, raped, abandoned, her shoe found in a deserted parking lot. Her father was dead from cancer. Her brother had gone off to the States. It was just the girl and her mother. *"Las muertas de Juárez,"* Manuel said. "There are ghosts everywhere. Socorro comes finding."

"Finding?" Drake asked.

"I mean to say looking."

"For what?"

"For her sister's spirit."

"But why does she think she'll find it here?"

"Because her sister passed this way each day on her way home from her *horchata* stand. And because this is a church, where spirits live."

There was silence then, and beyond that silence the sound of Corey gathering up some crowd, the sound of Jazzy saying, "You should join the circus." But then I heard Drake asking questions again. Drake still close, talking to Manuel.

"So why doesn't she come inside?" he asked. "Why won't she come past the gate?"

"Time, in my country, is the future, Drake. Socorro will come when she is ready."

There was grime on the floor of the bathroom, mud in a dark halo around the drain. I stripped off my stiff clothes and stood beneath a thin stream, thinking of Socorro and the ghost she was chasing. Of a sister, abandoned. Of the future of time.

❦

Watermelon juice in plastic jugs. Baskets of chips. Plates of wedged lime. A soup thickened by chicken and squash, and Lobo running in circles with his ears pulled high. The men in the folding chairs on the neighboring roof lit their cigarettes and laughed; and it was understood, by all of us by then, that we'd become their entertainment, that they would miss us when we were gone.

Mr. Thom was telling a story about a child he'd met on the work site that day—a boy who was nine who was home alone with his younger siblings all day while his parents worked at a *maquiladora* that was, the boy said, three bus rides away. "The boy seemed proud," Mr. Thom said, "of the care that he was giving. As if he were honored, not burdened, by the responsibility. I don't think, growing up, that I'd have been like that. I don't see it where I live; do you?"

"No," Mrs. K. said. "Not often. Or at least not often enough."

I thought about Kev, but the comparison didn't fit. I'd turned the word *responsibility* into a bad thing in my life. This boy, this squatters' village boy, had turned it, according to Mr. Thom, into something over which to be proud.

"He introduced me to his sister," Mr. Thom was saying. "She couldn't have been more than three. She wanted to help with the construction."

"Something like that happened to me," Catherine said. "I was taking a break, right? From all that shoveling. And I turned around, and there was this kid handing a bottle of Gatorade to me. I was, like, pretty embarrassed, because two minutes before, I'd been complaining to Mariselle. Like, what? A little shoveling's supposed to kill me?"

Mariselle said, "You weren't complaining *that* much, Catherine."

"Well. You know. Enough."

I was avoiding Riley by watching Drake—watching him take the conversation in while the sky above us changed. He didn't seem the least inclined to talk, but he was precise in the way that he listened. Tall and broad, he clearly came from more money than most of the rest of us, but he wasn't arrogant. His head was in some other place. Increasingly, I wondered about the things he never shared.

Leonor and Concha were collecting the empty bowls of soup. They were bringing out trays of sliced green melon and bowls of M&M's. Corey was balancing a spoon on his nose, and even Mack was watching. Mr. Thom was shaking his head. Sophie was trying to one-up Corey, tossing the M&M's high and catching them with her mouth, like a seal at a fancy water park. You could get lost in it even if you weren't part of it, which is why I didn't hear the screams at first. Didn't hear Socorro, out in the street, in the shadows of that dusk.

What I noticed was Lobo's frenzy. Then I noticed Drake—pushing back from the table and running for the gate. The goose from across the street had gotten loose. Its wings were stretched and high and angry, its hard, yellow beak was snapping, and Socorro was there, her head in her hands, her body crouched low to the street. The wings were taller than she was, the white, assaulting wings.

"Get me the keys," Drake called, and Manuel, halfway to the gate himself, tossed them, and Drake caught them. In one swift motion he opened the door and rushed the goose, which swiveled its head about its ropy, white neck and, confused, beat its wings harder, unwilling to leave the girl, for whatever reason she'd been chosen, but made afraid, too—you could see it—by Drake's imposing height. The girl was crying now, sobbing, and the old lady from across the street was out on her porch waving a cane in the scene's direction, whether at the goose or at the girl I couldn't tell.

Drake never stopped. He just kept at the goose, closing in, raising his arms as if he could lasso the wild wings that way. Manuel was near, Manuel was yelling, but it was Drake from whom the goose finally fled, Drake who carried the girl through the gate, which Manuel closed and locked behind them. The girl was tiny, a wisp in an olive-colored dress with a crown of silky black hair.

Leonor was there with a bucket of ice, Mrs. K. at Leonor's side. Drake kept speaking, words that none of us could hear. He never let her down.

"God-damned goose," Jon said, and Mariselle said, "Really."

Riley looked as if she might cry.

That night, in the room up the unsteady flight of stairs, we all lay quiet. Everyone lost in her own thoughts, in the aftermath of Socorro, the goose, Drake, Manuel, who, in the end, extracted the child from Drake's arms and took her down the street to where she lived with a mother who had lost one daughter and could not afford to lose another. Socorro had not once lifted her head to look at us. She had only clung to Drake, sensing in him a safe harbor, a place where she could be afraid and then not afraid.

Time passed—there was no telling how much—and then, above me, I heard Riley turn. I saw her pale, lean arm fall down toward mine, a sheen in a black room, a hope I shouldn't have had.

"Hey," I whispered. "You awake?"

Nothing.

"Ri?"

She withdrew her arm. There was silence.

Mrs. K. had begun to snore—soft little whimpers that seemed embarrassed of themselves. Somebody deeper into the dark was jittery. I had the taste of dust far back in my throat, and when I swallowed, it was like swallowing over pebbles.

"Ri. Listen. This is stupid."

I turned on my left side and faced the wall. I turned

right, toward the door. I remembered the time that Kev had started crying late at night when my parents were out at some function and how I'd let him cry until I had to find out what was wrong. I'd gone into his room and found him balled up on one side, beneath a twist of covers.

"Hey," I'd said, "what's going on?"

"Can you sit with me, Georgia?" he'd asked. "Can you?"

So I'd sat with him, on the side of his bed, waiting for his breathing to steady and his limbs to relax, for the covers to go looser over him. I'd just sat there, waiting. When my parents got home I was still sitting there, listening to the sound of my little brother sleeping.

seven

We'd stirred up fifteen batches of concrete; Sam and Corey had traded off being our wheelbarrow men. We'd mixed enough to pour two thirds of the bathroom floor and to supply the sewage hole crew besides; by now they were slapping the stuff between the concrete blocks like old-time bricklaying pros. Mack had said that we'd work an hour more, get the floor all poured so that it could set while we hammered up the framing come tomorrow. My arms were like noodles; my head hurt. My secondhand scrubs were soaked through. Mariselle and Mrs. K. built up another cement-and-gravel mound. Then they flattened the top and poured the water in, and Jon and I stirred.

We made four more batches of that concrete, and that's when things changed—that's when the wind began to blow and Sophie, noticing, said: "The gods are showing mercy." She pulled her T-shirt out away from her chest to get some breeze against her skin, and now Catherine was looking up—removing her sunglasses and squinting toward the sky. Her body was perfectly straight and, even in all that heat, somehow cool and orderly, and when I saw her staring, I followed her gaze. Saw the clouds off in the distance, nowhere near the sun. The sky itself was less blue than green, even without sunglasses on. At the big hole Riley was noticing; the Anapra kids, perched high on the cliffs, had their eyes tilted skyward, too.

Now the green that had been creeping in turned a seaweed color. There was the spitting of something against my face, the hard sound of gravel on my glasses, which wasn't rain but sand.

There were flutters on the cliff, on Lupe's roof, on the monkey bars—splashes of kids climbing down, as the bigger ones handed the littler ones to the ground.

The girl with patent leather shoes went running for Drake, who was in the sewage hole slopping the concrete mix between the blocks. She leaned toward him, waved.

We were calling *"¡Adiós!"* as the kids scattered—their shirts and dresses blowing, their strawberry, mango, lemon, peach colors flaring against the sky. Mrs. K. turned her back to another gust of wind. I felt the sand blow hard, knock against my shins. The blue tarp that had been hung over the lumber pile crackled and snapped, tried to tear away from its posts.

"Anything loose goes off the ground and into the shed," Mack called; and now we were scrambling to get our stuff out of the storm—the bags of cement, the gravel, the shovels, the rakes, the buckets—leaving the block right where it was but hauling up the plywood planks on which we'd been mixing the concrete.

With every back and forth to Roberto's shed the wind kicked harder. Covering our eyes with our hands, covering our mouths, we bent against it. The sky was like pea soup, and finally one fat cloud caught up with the sun; and when I looked back down to the streets of Anapra, there were no colors, just blobs of tumbleweed knocking around between the shanties. I made out a mule at the other end of town trying to snap itself free from a rope tied to a fence. I saw the shells of old junker cars ripple with wind. It was like a scene from one of Geoff's video games, and I wanted to take photographs. But now Mack was saying that we had to get inside, and we were running, tripping to the banging open door of Lupe's kitchen. It slammed behind Mrs. K., the last one in. It didn't matter that we'd come inside. I felt the prickles of sand on my skin.

There was room at the one window for just some of us to see, and Jazzy was already there with Catherine, their hair gone wild with the wind and hanging down their backs like curtains. Soon they joined the crowd that had collected and knotted around Sam, who went nowhere without a deck of cards. Those who weren't dealt in watched Corey to see what he'd do with his Hacky Sack.

Outside, the sand was blowing up and falling down like hail, slapping the thin metal roof. But still it hadn't rained; and even Mack seemed surprised, or at least he didn't use the occasion to give us some you-see-what-I've-been-talking-about instruction. He was watching over the shoulders of Drake, who now stood at the window. I thought about the mule down the road, wondered if it had gotten itself free, and if it had, where was it going? Where do Anapra mules go?

Finally Drake spoke, and when he did, all of us but Corey turned. "Houses down there can't survive this wind," he said. "It's like they're getting clobbered by snow." Suddenly I wanted to see what Drake was seeing—stand next to him to wait out the storm. There was room by the window, and I stepped in beside him. Neither of us spoke for quite a while. The sand, harassed by the wind, was a truly putrid shade of green. An old pickup truck had stopped in its tracks, letting the wind and the sand whip all around it. A flattened cardboard box had separated from four walls of tin and was pinwheeling across the sand.

"Jesus," I said. The snakes of electrical wires shimmied, as if they were being snapped by an invisible hand.

"They make the storms different here," Drake said. "I've seen this kind of thing only one time before when I was twelve."

"Where?"

"Hilton Head Island. My dad has a place."

Beyond the window a wheelbarrow rumbled loose from a shed near the top of a hill and started to wobble backward. It crashed into a bucket fence, and then the buckets started rolling. "So, what was it like?" I asked. "That storm, I mean?"

"Brutal. Came up quick, when there were lots of people still on the beach. Picked up buckets, hats, towels; tossed them. Pulled the waves up high and crashed them, too."

"Where were you?"

"Standing on my dad's balcony. Beachfront home." He said it as if it were something to apologize for, as if he were ashamed of his family's wealth. I'd met lots of rich kids, growing up on the Main Line. But never one like Drake.

"How long did the storm last?" I asked him.

"Too long."

"I guess."

"A girl drowned."

"I'm sorry."

"She lived five houses down from my dad. She was six. She'd gone out to play while the nanny was sleeping. No one realized she was missing, and then it was too late."

I just stood there. I just stood and listened.

"Stuff like that happens, and it changes the way you think." On the other side of the window, the sand was howling at the monkey bars, throwing itself up against the metal like bullets made of spit.

"You were good with Socorro last night," I finally said.

"That goose," he said, "should have been on its leash."

"Or eaten."

Games were going on behind us, idle talk, pacing, Sam slapping out another game of cards. "This should have been rain," Mariselle was saying. "That's what they need."

I turned and registered her concern, decided that she was, after all, a girl with a heart, the kind of complicated heart that it might make sense to know.

"Drake," Mack said, "Roberto needs you in the kitchen."

Drake gave me a perplexed look, then turned, leaving me alone at the window before the spectacle of the storm. That was when I remembered that I hadn't seen Riley, that I'd lost track of her in all the commotion.

I scanned the room, the knots of people—Mrs. K. and Mr. Thom at one table, Catherine and Jazzy by the door, Sam and most of the rest of them jammed around a game of hearts. Corey and Jon were sitting side by side, backs against the table, Corey teaching Jon some juggling trick; and nowhere in any of that was Riley.

"You seen Riley, Corey?" I asked. He shook his head no without lifting his eyes from the Hacky Sacks. I scanned the room again: no Riley. I started walking the hard-dirt floor now, checking the worn-out benches, thinking maybe Riley was napping, but nothing. I wasn't supposed to care, she wasn't even talking to me now, but I was worried—I couldn't help it; I didn't see Riley. "Mack, you seen Riley?" I finally asked him when he returned from the kitchen with Drake.

He pointed his chin in the direction of Lupe's stove, and I didn't understand. Then he thrust it out in the same direction, and I went that way—toward the counter where the food was served, toward the stove. There was a door back there that I hadn't seen before. It wasn't latched. I pushed against it. It opened to a room that was hardly any wider than the cot it contained.

"Riley?" I asked. "Ri?" She was lying there, with her hair sprawled out around her. She was holding Lupe's one outstretched hand. The other hand she'd given to Sophie.

"Hey," I said in the softest voice.

Sophie turned and gave me the please-be-quiet eye.

"What's up?" I asked, trying to lower my voice, too, trying not to give away my rising panic, because panic is contagious. It's worse than a disease.

"I don't know," Sophie said. "Something about her head—it's hurting." Lupe's hand was so big compared to Riley's. So dark and wrinkled with age. "Mack said I could take her back here, get her to rest. Lupe's being an angel."

"Well, that was nice of Mack," I said; and now what had been becoming panic geared into relief, and now the relief was a little like anger, and I was standing there feeling pissed. Pissed that Sophie was there beside Riley, who hadn't opened her eyes or said a thing. "And nice of Lupe, too." Scared, too. Mostly I was scared.

"Real nice of Lupe," Sophie said. "I mean, this is her room."

I nodded again in Lupe's direction. I took off my glasses and cleaned them, then fitted them back onto my nose. Took a long breath, as if I thought I could wait out Sophie and her ministrations.

"Well, how is she now?"

"I don't know. Says she's still kind of hurting and dizzy."

"Storm's huge," I said, trying to sound casual, "and mean. You should see it outside. We won't be going anywhere soon." Between Lupe and Sophie and Riley, the room was full. I stood in the doorway, feeling monstrous.

"I think we should just let her sleep," Sophie said, looking for a long time at Riley, then glancing at me. Telling me without telling me that it'd be good for me to leave.

"Sure," I said. "Right. Check on you soon."

"I'll let you know if she needs anything."

"Uh-huh."

"But I kind of doubt it. I think she just needs sleep."

Sophie the nurse. As if she knew a damned thing. As if she had any idea what was wrong, as if she could fix it. I closed the door behind me. Breathed.

eight

Two hours later, when the sandstorm stopped, it was as if the whole world had been smeared. It took us an hour more to dig out our two vans, to start bumping down the road. It was true what Drake had said. It was as if Anapra had been hit with snow. There were pieces of tin and mattresses all tossed out to the street, parts of walls that had folded, cracked pots, a rubber wheel that had gotten loose from some bike and was wobbling around. The mule was gone. The doll that I'd seen tossed up on the roof was nowhere to be found. The kids of Anapra were wherever they had vanished to.

I sat taking photos of the things that still remained the whole way back.

Riley rode with her eyes shut tight and her head on Sophie's shoulder.

nine

That night, after dinner, most of us went straight to bed. Even Corey packed up his Hacky Sacks and slipped away for sleep. It was everything we'd seen and done. It was thinking about those kids in their blown-out shacks, and the mule and the doll—things vanished and buried and broken—and tomorrow the people of Anapra would open their doors to the blaring sun and begin making everything right again. Hammering the roofs back above their heads. Straightening the pipes. Finding the mule. Hanging the signs.

"Night, Riley," I whispered to the above-me bunk.

Nothing but nothing floated down.

The air seemed heavier than ever, thickened by the storm. When I breathed or swallowed, I felt the gravel in a clot by my tonsils. When I closed my eyes, I saw color. When I opened them, I saw storm. I saw Riley lying on that cot in that minuscule room, Lupe and Sophie on either side. I saw Drake at the window and me next to Drake, my hand on his forearm.

"Stuff like that happens, and it changes the way you think," Drake had said, as if he took his own decency for granted, as if it were inevitable—but decency never is, decency is as close as you get to impossible; and if I were decent, I thought, if I truly were, I'd stop letting Riley run from her problems. I wouldn't let her disappear; I wouldn't let her pretend to some girl who hardly knew her that she'd gotten smacked by some headache that a sweet nap might cure. I would insist. Out loud. In the open. I'd do something at last with the panic in my head, save Riley even though it seemed she had precious little interest in saving herself. I'd out her secret, for her sake.

I sat up, slipped from between my sheets, grabbed my camera, found my way to the door. I stood out on the balcony beneath the silver fish of the moon, inhaling and exhaling slowly. I thought about Riley and that punk word *average*, how Riley's answer to that had been to starve herself to excessive thin. Extremes aren't average. But neither was Riley ever anything like average: She could draw an old man or a pair of boots from memory; she could take beads and string them into sunsets; she could just sit there looking like her Riley self with a mist of freckles and her percussion earrings and anyone would stop to see her, anyone would. She was letting her mother's word rule. She was letting her secret destroy her. I was Riley's best friend, and I'd done nothing but cower. I'd vanished, too, as big as I was.

The men on the neighboring roof had fallen asleep. I could see their chins tipped onto their chests, their profiles lit up by the moon. I began dialing back through the photos, each trapped splinter of Juárez. The children who had nothing, smiling; the mothers who were holding their hands. Privilege doesn't make you smarter. It doesn't gift you decency.

Below me now I heard the scratch of Lobo's nails on the courtyard floor, saw his tail swatting the air. My hair was a mess; my feet were naked; I went to see what the lone wolf was up to. Every loose plank wobbled and walloped, no matter how lightly I trod.

"Hey, Lobo," I called when I reached solid ground.

"Georgia?" My name rose from the shadows; but all I saw was the slatted dark, the strange nighted shadows of Manuel's makeshift courtyard. When my eyes adjusted, I realized it was Drake, sitting in one of those plastic beach chairs, his hand on Lobo's head. Too late, I thought, to turn back. Too late, and I didn't want to.

"Hey," I said.

"Lobo," he said, "seemed nervous. I came out to see what was up."

I glanced at Lobo, then back at Drake—the straight drop of his cheeks to his jaw, the short, unambiguous nose, the wide, smooth plane of his brow. He wasn't looking at me, not really. He was looking at something only he could see—looking at it or searching for it, roaming. There was room for me in all of that, and so I stood there, waiting.

"So what *is* up?" I asked.

"I don't know. But definitely something is."

The moon was big; it was so close, I could have

grabbed it. It was shadow and it was light, quiet and loud with itself.

"There's an extra chair," Drake said, "if you want to hang."

"Yeah," I said. "Thanks." The chair creaked as I settled in. Lobo wheezed like a saw on a torrefied log. There was a small bulb of light outside the door to Manuel's room. Drake just kept staring at the sky.

"Hard to think," he said, "that the same moon is hanging above the Main Line right now."

"One world, one moon," I said.

"Yeah," he said. "Except not really."

Lobo whined, settled down, cushioned his head on his legs. It was hard here, and it was easy at home. It wasn't one world, and we both knew it.

"You know Jack Gilbert?" I asked. "The poet?"

"Yeah," Drake said, after a minute. "Actually, I do."

"'We find out the heart only by dismantling what / the heart knows,'" I said. "Gilbert's words."

Drake just shook his head. He might have laughed, but his voice was muffled. Lobo's ears went up on alert, and Drake put his hand out to calm him. Now I was looking at Drake and seeing moons in his eyes, and seeing the ruin in the moons in those eyes but also a gentling, too, a clear shot at healing.

"I like the line," I said. "Even if I don't have it figured out."

"I think it's about starting fresh," Drake said after a long time had passed. "Your line. Seeing things newly."

"Maybe." Up in the sky, a second generation of stars had washed up on the shore of the moon, or a cloud had passed, revealing. Lobo's tail was going back and forth, anxious, waiting. "What do you think Lobo sees?" I asked Drake.

"It's what he can see that we can't see that's got him worked up like he is."

I shook my head, didn't follow.

"The ghost," he went on. "That little girl who lost her sister. She's been looking for her sister's spirit. Maybe Lobo's gone and found it."

Upstairs, on the roof, a man had started snoring. The sound of dreams, I thought. The sound of survival.

"Manuel said that some nights after a storm has

passed over, he's almost sure he's caught a glimpse."

"Of what? Of Socorro's sister?"

"He didn't say exactly. Or if he did, I didn't understand. All I know is that a storm passed today. That Lobo's on edge. That you're here and I'm here, and all of us are waiting."

We sat there and said nothing—Drake's hand on the dog's head, Lobo going in and out of restful and alert. There is silence that stumbles toward words, and silence that transcends words. The skies change, and the truth does. But right then silence was the truth, the stars; silence was Drake; it was me breathing.

"Socorro's the only one left," Drake said. "She's five. She doesn't say much. But she doesn't give up looking."

A girl after your own heart, I thought; and suddenly it was clearer to me—why Drake had taken such an interest in the child. He had seen something in her that he'd recognized. He had leaned toward it. Time is the future in Juárez. Friendship, too, lives in the future and not only the past.

"What would the ghost of Socorro's sister look like?" I asked now. "I mean, what do you think?"

"Something that floats," Drake said. "That's all I can figure."

I smiled. "Like what that floats?"

"I don't know—sailboats, balloons, kites, happiness. . . ."

"Happiness?"

"Just an idea I had. Probably stupid."

I looked around in the dark for something floating. I saw angles, stucco, a hoisted cross, dust-dirtied windows, the belly of the splintery stairs, the men on the rooftop sleeping.

"Can I ask you a question?" Drake said.

"Yeah?"

"Aren't you supposed to be sleeping?"

"Too much stuff," I said, "in my head."

He let it go at that; he didn't press, but suddenly I wanted to tell him. Suddenly I didn't want to be alone with me—the regrets I had, the things I'd broken. "You know anything about panic attacks?" I asked him finally.

He turned, looked at me, shook his head.

I settled back into my chair, closed my eyes. "I had my first almost two years ago. They're like heart attacks, but not really. They're like wanting to run except for the fact that you're stuffed stupid and trapped inside the hole of yourself."

"You were having a panic attack? Just now? Upstairs?" It wasn't an accusation, it wasn't gossip, the way Drake said it. It was just somebody trying to understand.

"I was trying not to," I said.

Drake watched me. He listened. Lobo had started to wheeze again, the ears like darts on his head. "I think happiness is the color white," he said after a long time.

I laughed—I don't know why; it just came out. "Why white?"

"I don't know. Peace. The truce you make with yourself."

I looked at Drake through the dark, his big hand on that dog's head.

"Georgia, you know the girl who I told you about? The one who drowned in the storm?"

I nodded, but it didn't matter. Drake had again fixed his eyes high on the moon, which a cloud had started to gauze over.

"I always thought I should have saved her. That I

should have *seen* her, you know, out there swimming. That I should have seen her drowning coming."

"That couldn't have been your fault," I said.

"It doesn't matter. She died. I was there." Lobo lifted his snout and moaned. There was a long silence after that.

"Happiness is the color of a truce," I said.

"Maybe," Drake said. "I hope so."

ten

The goose woke everybody else. It started honking soon after the first parabola of sun appeared from behind the mountains that rose beyond the compound; and it didn't stop until Lobo answered bark for honk—stood at the gate with his nose between the pickets.

I'd fallen asleep in that plastic chair and awakened to sunrise. Manuel's bulb was out, and the courtyard was going live—smoke rising through the kitchen windows, Jon and Neil creeping from the chapel's dark shell, Mrs. K. creaking down the stairs and heading for the bathroom, her hair mashed at embarrassing angles. Catherine opened the kitchen door and stood in the courtyard—arms crossed and eyes on the sun, refusing to take in her mother. Jazzy was singing—I heard her voice but couldn't see her. Not far from me, their legs straddling a wooden bench, Sophie and Riley sat face-to-face. Riley's pouch of bracelets was upended between them, and Riley had her back to me. It didn't matter: She had to have walked right by me, had to have seen me sleeping there, had to have known that I'd wake to this—her and Sophie, her new best friend, making bracelet plans.

"You're a genius, Riley," I heard Sophie saying. One by one she pulled each bracelet to the sky, letting the sun stream through. "You could sell these in Hollywood, to the celebrities, I swear," Sophie continued. "You could be famous."

"They're just bracelets," Riley said; but she was laughing, her nose tilted in the direction of her own dangled jewelry, which was all blazed up and brightly fractured by the roaring-over-Juárez sun. Riley really did have a gift for color. For making glass look like diamonds, rubies, gold.

"*Just* doesn't do you justice, girl. *Just* is not what these are."

"Bracelets don't get you into college, Sophie."

"You don't meet celebrities in college." Sophie caught my eye and smiled. "At least not most of the time."

I couldn't tell if Sophie knew that a fight was on, that she was sitting in the line of fire. *Turn around, Riley,* I tried to will her with my thoughts. *Turn around and let me back in.* But Riley wouldn't budge, and Sophie kept talking, kept pulling one bracelet after the other to the sky and telling Riley what a genius she was.

"So, like, what's next?" Sophie was asking. "What's the distribution plan?"

"Anapra," Riley said.

"Brilliant," Sophie said. "Swear to God."

Riley sighed, settled her head into the palm of one hand, settled her elbow onto the splintered picnic table. "So many kids" is what she finally said.

"And you'll be the girl," Sophie said, "who won't be forgotten."

The chapel door opened, and there was Mack, the brash streaks in his hair made even more aggressive by the sun. There, too, was Drake—a little beside, a little behind him. Together they were hoisting some ancient-looking toolbox, Mack staggering more than Drake, both of them headed for Mr. Thom's van. I couldn't see what Drake was seeing, where he was looking, if he was looking for me.

"Hey," I called.

"Hey." He was synced with Mack; he kept moving. I felt hulking ugly in my WITNESS PROTECTION T-shirt. My bare feet and my gym shorts.

"Need some help?" It was Sam, leaning out of the kitchen window.

"We're good," Mack said, though I could see how his muscles were tensing. "We're out of here in thirty minutes, guys. Make sure you're ready by eight." Mack and Drake kept making their way until finally they'd arrived at the van, where Mr. Thom had flung the back door wide and where the three of them now battled the box into place.

"Anything actually in working order in there?" Mr. Thom asked doubtfully, rubbing one hand over the box when they were done.

"Elbow grease," Mack said, "is a prerequisite." He

slammed the door shut, clapped the dust off his hands. He turned and took us in—Sam, still hanging out a kitchen window; Mrs. K.; Catherine, with one arm across the shoulder of Leonor, who had come to see what the hassle was about and who had stayed—a wide, pickety grin on her creased brown face.

Mrs. K. started saying that she could use a good masseuse; and right then is when Mariselle appeared, as if the courtyard were a theater—pacing a circle, reciting some dream, going on for the benefit of no one.

"Like, there was this wall," she was saying, "and I couldn't get over the wall, so I kept running, you know, right beside the wall so that I could find its end, but it never ended." She paced, but it was her eyes that were shifting back and forth, as if they were running after the dream. "I don't think I ever got to the end of the wall," Mariselle said. "I'm not sure, but I don't think so." Now she stopped and leaned against the second van. She crossed her eyes and squinted. "I'm trying to remember," she said, "if I got to the end of the wall."

We were waiting for more, for some decision about the dream; but Mariselle was done. She pulled herself up into a dead halt, lifted her head, shook her hair out, and smiled.

"Well, thank you for sharing," Mrs. K. said, and for some reason that made Riley laugh—the old, familiar Riley laugh. Then Sophie was laughing, and Mrs. K., too, and even Catherine couldn't help herself. Only Jazzy appeared to be confused—Jazzy who, I finally figured out, had been sitting above us this whole time, taking in the scene from the balcony. Taking it in, but clearly not hearing a word.

"What's so funny?" she demanded.

"Mrs. K. is doing stand-up," Sophie called to her. She lifted one hand, and Riley high-fived her; and then they both broke into rioting, ricocheting giggles. It was enough. I stood. I was decamping. I didn't have to stand there watching while Riley pretended that I did not exist.

"Georgia." I heard my name and turned. "You ever get some sleep?" It was Drake, the quietest large person I'd ever seen. Drake, pushing the hair from his eyes.

"Some," I said. "I guess. In the beach chair. I guess." I cast a furtive glance at my ghostly T-shirt.

"Moon beach."

"Something like that."

He smiled, but his eyes were still tunnels I couldn't see through. They were bastion places that held out promise for some light. I stood in that sun. I looked for that light. I stood there undecided and confused.

"Thought of another Gilbert poem," Drake said. "Thought of this line: 'We must risk delight.'"

"'A Brief for the Defense,'" I said. "One of my teacher's favorite poems. Buzzby. That was the guy's name. He practically drove me insane, but still, it turned out that the man had impeccable taste."

"Fierce," Drake said. He hardly moved when he talked. Didn't use his hands. Didn't shift his feet.

"'We must have / the stubbornness to accept our gladness in the ruthless / furnace of this world.'" It was my favorite line from the Gilbert poem. I'd never recited it to a soul. Didn't know anyone else, except for Buzzby, who'd have even cared.

"Yo." Now it was Jon, calling from the threshold of the courtyard kitchen, megaphoning his hands around his mouth. "Leonor's cooked up about a million eggs. Sam'll chow them all down if we let him."

I looked from Sam to Mrs. K. to Mariselle to Sophie

to Drake. "Tour leaves in twenty-five minutes," Drake said. He turned for the kitchen. I looked beyond him, to Sophie and Riley—to Riley, actually, who was facing my way, giving me the oddest stare.

"You're a stealth operator, Walker," she said. Then she pivoted back, and the delicate frame of her delicate back was like a door that had pulled itself shut.

I felt it then—felt something inside me snap. "What is with you, Ri?" I said; and I didn't care if Sophie was watching or if Mack was nearby, if Jazzy was floating, headed for the kitchen wearing the shortest pair of short shorts. It was getting stupid, this whole thing was—why couldn't Riley see? Why was she so flipping insistent on barricading me?

"You know what I miss?" Riley said now, loud for Sophie's sake—a one-woman exclusionary act. She lifted a hand to the plane above her eyes to block the sun, and the shadow cast by the crook of her arm looked like one of these triangles you play in music class.

"What do you miss?" Sophie asked. She was looking at me and then at Riley. She looked at Jazzy, who seemed flummoxed.

"My long, white, scrubbed-clean bathtub." Riley

was stuffing her stash of bracelets back inside her pouch. She was unstraddling the bench, standing up.

"Don't start on that."

"God," Riley said. "I'd fall asleep in it. I'd soak all day and not get out."

"Like your mother," I said, and Riley glared. Sophie went on, because what did Sophie know? She was just some pawn in Riley's game.

"Don't start dreaming, though," Sophie said. "Today isn't bath day. Today is framing."

"Yeah. Whatever that means."

"You take a two-by-four and a two-by-four and a two-by-four until you have yourself a wall."

"Hammer and nails."

"Correct."

"I've never even hammered a nail."

"Today's your lucky day."

The sun was a full red circle out there above the mountains and climbing fast. The day was getting on. Eight o'clock.

"Leonor's made eggs," I said, the words like metal between my teeth.

"Eggs," Riley said, crinkling her nose.

"I'm serious," I said, and I was. "Seriously, Ri. Breakfast."

"Vans leave in twelve minutes," Mack called. He'd had his head inside the van's wide engine, and now he was slamming shut the hood, returning a wrench to Manuel. "Weather," he said to Mr. Thom. "Chokes these engines every time." Then he turned to me and gave me a look that I understood to mean *No more bitching right now.*

Riley's sapphire eyes were cool and hard. She stared through me, then walked past and up those stairs, into that cavern of a room. She defied me to defy her, and I wouldn't. I went up the stairs right after her. Changed in silence, my broad back to hers.

eleven

We drove to Anapra with American music playing loud. Drake had rigged his iPod to the van's third-rate audio system and turned the volume to high; and he'd done it with Mack's permission, because, I guess, looking back on it now, Mack was trying to keep things light. To cool the fight. To get back to business. To plant seeds, not uproot them.

The music was our own; it was loud, but that wasn't the amazing part. The amazing part was that Drake sang, and that he was no way shy about it. Sitting in the middle of the rest of us, he did beatbox, rap, hip-hop, three songs in a row from Maroon 5. He had a voice you wouldn't believe could come from a guy his make and size, from a guy who'd been so good at being quiet. Even the guys in the van were giving him respect. Corey, too, the Hacky Sack king, was giving it up for the Third.

"Dude," he said, "where you been hiding that thing? You should have talked more, man, given us some warning."

Drake didn't mind the praise, didn't need it. He just sang as if he'd grown up singing, as if the music weren't just for him or for us but for all of Anapra, too—for survivors of sandstorms, of deserts, of murders that go unsolved. "The ruthless furnace of this world." I'd have recorded his singing with my camera if I could. I'd have sent it back, across the Rio Grande, past the border guards, way past El Paso, home. To be played at night. To restore myself.

There were signs, all along the road, of yesterday's storm. Walls that had shimmied down, big pileups of tumbleweed, so many squares of corrugated tin that had snapped off houses or shops and lay wherever the wind had left them. The closer we got to Anapra, the more banks of sand we saw, or gutters of nothing where the wind had tunneled through. There were bottles rolling around in the streets. Loose dogs chasing kicked-in metal trash cans.

When we turned left into Anapra, we saw the people fighting back—women and girls with brooms, some boys, too, pushing the sand out of their front doors and into the side yards or out onto the street. What had been blown away was being carried back—mothers, fathers, little kids with tires lifted above their heads, pallet boxes, ceramic pots, tarps. Sticks were being bundled. An entire clothesline had been freshly pinched with plastic clips. One kid had an armful of paper. The mule had made its way back home.

The dogs traveled in packs. One gang of them picked up their heels after Mr. Thom's van, which was itself kicking up so much sand, it looked as if the dogs were going up in smoke. Drake had stopped singing by now, and I'd taken out my camera. If my mom had seen this, she'd have found the right words. All I would ever have was pictures.

"I am never," Mariselle said, "ever, ever complaining about taking out the trash again."

"You got it, sister," Sophie said.

"I mean, like"—and then Mariselle sighed, but it was a perfectly reasonable sigh.

"What makes it so that they don't up and quit?" Sophie asked.

"This is their life," Mrs. K. said. "They make the best of it."

I was taking photograph after photograph. I was looking into the houses where the doors had been blown off, remembering the women who had never made it home—who had been taken, vanished, disappeared, never to come back to this, their home. I was thinking how too-small the houses were for grieving; how a daughter might have waited up all night, all day, all night again for a mother to return. How a sister might. Socorro. And then what? And then how do you make the best of that? And what do you say to all the other daughters, and how do you keep your loved ones safe? How do you keep standing up when you're shaken to the bone?

"We're going to have to dig out before we start framing," Mack was saying from up front as the van hit the sand hills hard and bumped us down the road.

We nodded behind him.

"We saw yesterday what the wind could do," he continued. "We all know what we're coming back to. Some of you will be cleaning out the sewage hole. Some will sweep the foundation. The lumber is under the tarp, but we're going to have to go find that tarp. The sand will be heavy, and you know it's hard work. Spare each other. Don't forget your water bottles."

"Hammering is starting to sound pretty good," Riley leaned Sophie's way and said. She flexed her right arm and scared up no muscle.

We were put into teams, guys and girls—Riley and Drake, of all couplings, to begin with. He was huge to her small, but Mack said that was the point—to work each other's strength and cancel out each other's weakness. "Mismatches can be misleading" is what he said. "We've only got this morning to make this place right if we want to stay on schedule."

Riley had propped her pouch of bracelets near the water cooler. She had looked at me when she was paired with Drake, raised her eyebrow—a Riley triumph. But the thing was, I had no claim on him; I'd only sat beside him talking. Only traded Jack Gilbert lines. You can want something more than you can say. That doesn't ever mean it's yours.

In the shed, Roberto and Lupe were ready with the tools, handing them off to us. We marched through the sand in our assigned pairs. I'd gotten paired with Sam, who had tied his unruly hair back with one bandana and knotted another one around his neck. He managed, he'd said once, his school's baseball team. He had a mind for statistics and a coxswain's body; but he worked—I had already noticed this—as hard as anybody else, making up for what he lacked in brawn with a pretty intense determination.

"You have a weakness?" Sam had joked when Mack put us together.

"Not one," I'd said grimly. "And you?"

"Just don't want to show you up," he said, "in the bucket-hoisting department." He lifted an eyebrow over a very green eye and laughed. I laughed, too, because that's another thing about panic: Distractions sometimes scare it off. Laughter you force yourself into. There'd be no fixing what was wrong between Riley and me—not today, not in Anapra, not beneath that sun. I grabbed a bucket and Sam seized a shovel, and we headed off to where we knew the lumber was—beneath layers and layers of sand. It was like February snow where we came from, only the heaped-up sand smoked every time it was touched. It started out with Sam shoveling and me holding the bucket, but I kept getting overcome with the dust.

"Here," Sam said, and he showed me where to stand so that the dust would blow right past me and not straight into my lungs. He was a statistician; that's what he'd told us. But he had a mind for tactics, too, which was the reason, I realized, that he won every time he pulled out his deck of cards.

We talked while we worked—about his baseball team, how they'd made it to districts even after their star pitcher tore a ligament, then lost on the run-up to states. I tried to picture Sam out in the dugout with his clipboard and cap, marking pitches and strikeouts and errors and hits on some official pad, getting called on by the coach for some key fact. But Sam wasn't half bad at the shoveling, either—in fact, he made it seem easy. He had this nice, smooth way of digging and lifting, nothing extra in his effort. The sand, when Sam moved it, didn't look as if it weighed a thing.

"You're good at that," I told him.

"Yeah. And like you said, you have no weakness."

I hauled every bucket to the designated dump, right around the corner from Lupe's kitchen, not looking in Riley's direction, not giving her that—I couldn't. When I'd come back, Sam was ready with more. You couldn't tire him out; he just kept coming at you—the bandana at his neck soaked through with sweat.

By nine thirty some of the kids from the day before had returned, many in the same bright outfits. You wouldn't have known from their faces that they'd been through a storm. They were smiling, waving, pointing, climbing back up onto Lupe's roof and the monkey bars to get their bird's-eye view of our work. Someone had taken special care with Isabela's hair, which was cornrowed back, away from her face, each cornrow pinned with a bright pink clip. She wore the same orange tank top and no shoes. She stood shy, in the shade of Lupe's kitchen, until I yelled, *"Hola"*; and that was enough. She started running—jumping straight into my arms. Holding her high was like holding up air.

"¿Cómo estás?" I asked.

"Bien."

"Estamos construyendo un baño."

Isabela nodded. She touched her index finger to her mouth, then pointed to Lupe's kitchen. *"Mamá,"* she said, stretching her arm even farther; and I set her down, and she went flying. I waited to see if she'd come back to me, but she was gone for now.

By this time, more Anapra kids had taken their seats in the grandstands. There were rows of them now up on the bald hill, stitches of color on the rocks; and there were so many sitting on Lupe's roof that I worried there'd be some disaster. On the monkey bars six of them sat—the blue-eyed brothers, the boy with the strawberry-colored shirt, three girls I didn't remember seeing the day before.

"We're the next best thing to a Cinema Five," Sam said. I glanced about at the other GoodWorks teams, and I understood that Mack hadn't been half wrong when he paired us in our twos. The site was near to what it had been before the storm. We'd be able to frame that afternoon.

I could hear pots and pans being banged around in the kitchen, water running. I could hear Lupe talking with another woman, Roberto's voice working its way in, too. Lunch, I thought, and I thought about Riley. About how she'd have to eat today, about how I'd lost my place as the person who might help her.

Half an hour on, we were still working—digging, lifting, hauling. We'd stopped for the millionth time for water, and then Sam and I had started again; and now when I hauled the bucket around to the dump, I heard something besides pots and pans in the kitchen, some version of soft sadness. It was quick inhales and real fast exhales—a child, I realized, crying. Like the monster bird had fitted its wings inside a person much too small for panic. I emptied my bucket, went around to the kitchen door, stepped in out of the sun; it was Isabela. She was sitting on one of the long, wooden tables, big tears on her face. Seeing me, she started crying harder. I looked from her to Lupe.

"Mamá," Isabela was crying. *"Mamá."* She was pointing past the door where I was standing, to the high part of the road. Lupe was stroking the little girl's head, saying some quiet something in Spanish; but whatever she said just made the girl cry harder, and

finally Roberto, who was standing near, explained.

"Her mother," he said, pointing to where Isabela was pointing, "gone home. Fire on her hand. Bad burn. Isabela is scared. She wants to see her mother. Lupe has to stay to cook."

I stood in the doorway with the empty bucket in my hand. I thought about how quickly things can disappear, especially in Anapra, where stories like Socorro's were too common and where Isabela was crying even harder now, inconsolable, and where my own best friend had traveled far from me because I'd cared out loud. Through the window on the opposite wall, I saw Sam standing by the lumber pile, leaning on his shovel, waiting for me to return. I knew my options, and I weighed them. "I'll be right back," I told Roberto, and I stepped out into the sun and hurried around to my partner.

"You get lost?" Sam teased.

"Sorry. I—"

"I mean, here we were, winning the sand-hauling competition, and then what happens? You disappear."

"Didn't you hear Isabela crying?" I asked.

"No." The teasing stopped. He got serious.

"Roberto says that her mother got hurt working in Lupe's kitchen—a burn, I think, something with the fire. She went home and left Isabela here, and now Isabela is upset and she wants to get back to her house, and—you know—well, I thought I'd help her."

"I don't get it." He leaned on the handle of his shovel, watching me.

"I was thinking I might take Isabela home," I said, shifting in my sneakers. "So that she could see her mom, I mean. See that she's okay. That's she going to be, anyway."

"You know that Mack isn't going to like that," he said after a pause. "Nobody walks in Anapra alone."

"Right, yes. I know that. But if you came with me, I wouldn't be alone."

"What?"

"I mean, if we both went, would it be so bad?"

"Taking little girls home isn't in the job description, Georgia. It's also probably against the rules. Talk to Mack. He'll get someone to get Isabela home."

"But she trusts *me*," I said, and I know it sounded stupid, plaintive; I know it sounded like what it was: like me needing to be needed. Me, the one who had come all the way to Juárez to forfeit her best friend.

"You're kind of an odd one," Sam said, but he wasn't being mean when he said it.

"I know." I traced the sand with the toe of my heavy-duty sneaker, looked up, caught him smiling.

"I'll cover for you, if you want." He smiled more broadly. It was like getting permission for something we both knew was wrong.

"Could you?"

He gave me the long look of a statistician. He shrugged his shoulders. "Sure."

"I owe you big-time," I said.

"Yeah, Georgia. You're not kidding."

"I'll make it fast."

"Of course you'll make it fast. And don't be stupid, okay? Just go and then come back."

She wouldn't let me carry her; she had to lead the way. We cut across the deep sand on the opposite side of Lupe's kitchen, away from the teams of sand sweepers, then climbed a steep, sinking, sand-sucking pitch and got ourselves onto a road that swung high to the left. I kept saying her name, and she kept saying *"Mamá,"* and

I kept wishing that I could think of something useful and consoling.

The houses here were like the houses I had already seen, except that every single one was different. Across some of the pallet walls sheets of dark paper had been nailed. Across some front yards there was barbed wire. Between two houses tires had been planted straight up in the ground, and inside the tires there were sprouts of cacti. You could tell where the storm had been and what had already, just that morning, been repaired or dug out or hung on a line so that the sand would shake loose from the dresses, pants, sun-bleached slips. We passed ladies walking beneath little kids' umbrellas. We passed a group of boys playing something like soccer with a foam ball. There was a house built so squarely of cinder block that it reminded me of Riley's Rubik's cube, which she had never yet solved. There was a house that had been built of plastic stacking boxes, almost like something Kev would have Legoed, except for the bird in a cage by the front door, which was green and squawked as we passed. There were larger houses, nice, stucco houses that were painted the colors of seashore homes—turquoise, white, and pink—and out in the middle of the road was half a skull of a large dog, all its teeth lined up like piano keys, or maybe the skull had belonged to a small horse.

"Mamá," Isabela kept saying, tugging me along; and then she started running and I was running to keep up, her hand still in mine, so tiny.

We came to a house with real glass windows, a real front door, a dark green roof, three dogs in the yard, tied to a fence. It was the nicest house in all of Anapra, possibly, at least. All of a sudden I wanted it urgently for Isabela, wanted the door to open, wanted Isabela's mother to be standing there, calling Isabela home. But Isabela never even glanced in that direction. She kept tugging me forward, kept running. We went around a curve, across down-on-the-ground electrical wires. We dodged the stinking trickles of sewage. We passed a group of men, and I wondered if I had gone too far, why I hadn't asked for Mack's permission. Thought about how, if Riley and I were still best friends, she'd have noticed I was gone; she'd be on the lookout for my return. Then the broom truck went by, playing the kind of music they play on the horse show merry-go-round back home and kicking up a storm of dust, and

I thought about my dad and how he always said that sometimes you can't know what is right or wrong until you get some distance.

Finally Isabela broke free and turned right, up a hill. She ran with her arms stretched out, and her *"Mamá"* loud but growing softer as she ran away from me. She never looked back, never waved. I stopped and stood where I was and waited for a sign that the little girl was really home—that this was hers, this mostly-tin house with the one-pallet wall, the door made of a heavy black curtain and beside it a tall cactus that bloomed these bright red flowers. Someone drew the curtain aside. Isabela disappeared within. She had her proof, I hoped at least, that her mama would be fine.

I stood and waited for I don't know what more. Then I turned and walked the road alone. Listened to my feet on the slide of thick sand.

twelve

I returned the way I'd come, up along the high road, past the half skull, by the bird in the cage. The women with the umbrellas were down on a parallel road; and the broom truck was returning, dust high ahead and above and beside and behind it, but the music loud as ever. Three men had come out of one of the houses and were fixing a fence that had fallen in the storm. An old black dog lay in a stripe of shade, his head on his crossed-together paws. I walked as fast as I could until a pack of dogs started trotting slowly behind me. Dogs smell fear; that is what my father says. I tried to give off the scent of someone taking a pleasant little stroll.

But the closer I got to Roberto's compound, the more I felt the wobble of panic. Up in the bald hills above the site, the Anapra kids had gotten out of their crouch. They were standing, stretching out, as if to get a better view of something I couldn't see from where I was. On the roof of Lupe's kitchen, the same thing was true—kids on their feet, kids in tension. Something was broken; I knew something had gone wrong. The kids were on their feet, some with their hands over their mouths, all of them, but I couldn't guess why, couldn't parse the silence.

Apply your intelligence to every living thing. I heard my mother, and then I heard myself telling Drake that panic attacks are like wanting to run except that you can't because you are trapped inside the hole of who you are.

Don't you dare break down, I told myself, remembering Buzzby's class and Longwood Gardens, the night before Juárez. *Don't you dare.* And now I was running—kicking up dust in the face of the dogs, which made the dogs run, too, close at my heels, yipping. If they'd come any closer, they'd have had my ankles in their teeth, my shoelaces, something. But I wasn't letting them get any closer. I wasn't letting anything else get in my way—not the dogs, not the dust, not myself, not the blackbird that thundered and banged in the place of my heart.

I wasn't going to be beat by panic. Not this time. Not one time more.

Nobody was at any of the sand-clearing stations. It was much too still. All I could hear as I came around the bend was my own big feet *thwonk*ing the sanded-over road. I nearly stumbled down the pitch, caught myself, kept stumbling on toward Lupe's kitchen; it was like trying to walk through ocean waves, because the sand was so loose and so soft. Not even Lupe was in Lupe's kitchen. Through the window on the opposite wall I could a crowd gathered in a circle. I turned from the door and hurried around. Sam was the first to see me.

"It's Riley," he said, and now I put my hand on my heart to stop the wings that wanted to start flying.

"Let me see her," I insisted, still pushing forward, pressing in. Now Corey and Mariselle stepped aside and made me an alley, and I could see what they had all already seen—Riley down on the ground, her head in Sophie's lap, her right hand in Lupe's. Roberto and Drake were holding a piece of tarp above her head to keep her face in shadow. It cast a pale blue across her skin.

"What happened?" I asked, looking at Drake, trusting Drake to tell me the news, the damage; trusting myself to hold back the panic, to do the right thing, to focus only on my friend.

"She passed out, Georgia. She was standing there, giving the girls their bracelets. . . ."

"Their bracelets?" I glanced around, glanced up at the roof, saw flashes of Riley color sparking from the dark arms of little girls, saw the pouch near Riley's head empty. I looked at Sophie, and she shook her head, chewed her lip, tried not to let loose the tears in her eyes.

"Drake caught her," Sophie said. "I saw it. She would have fallen back, into the sewage ditch. She would have hit her head on the block."

Drake didn't deny or confirm. I looked back down at Riley. "Riley," I said, "can you hear me?"

"She isn't talking," Sophie said. "She hasn't opened her eyes, either."

Mrs. K. was dabbing Riley's forehead with a towel. Catherine was concerned and silent. Lupe was calm and steady, watching Riley like she'd watch a pot of stew, careful and expectant.

"Where's Mack?" I asked at last.

"Getting the van with Mr. Thom."

"Where are they taking her?"

"A clinic down the road."

"I don't understand," I said, but I did; and that was worse. They were taking my one-and-only best friend to a clinic in Anapra. She was sick and a million miles from home, and I had been gone when she fell.

Mack got the van backed in as close to Riley as he possibly could, Mr. Thom calling, "A little more, you've still got room; a little more; no; there, you've got it," until Mack pulled to a complete stop. We all stepped back then and gave Drake the room he needed to scoop Riley into his arms. It was as if he'd been built for this, as if he had been rescuing people all his life, shaping his arms into a cradle. He stooped, brought Riley up with him, didn't let her head snap back. We let him go with her; we gave him more room. Even I gave

Drake more room, because if unconsciousness is sleeping, then he knew how not to mess with her dreams. Drake got Riley to the van as I went ahead and slid into the middle row beside Sophie, because it was the two of us, Mrs. K. said, who should go with Drake, Mack, and Roberto to the clinic. The rest were to stay behind and work with Mr. Thom. We were to send word if we could.

None of us spoke on the way to the clinic. Nobody asked me where I'd been, not even Mack, who was driving somewhere between fast and slow—fast on the smooth stretches, slow over the long, hard humps of sand. We were heading for a part of Anapra we'd never been. I turned around, and all I could see of the compound were the little kids, still standing on Lupe's roof—Riley's genius on their arms.

Up front, Roberto had started pointing the way. Mack verified every turn in Spanish. *"Sí, sí,"* Roberto would say, and then they drove again in silence until more directions needed giving and confirming.

"Do we even know what's wrong?" Sophie finally asked. "I mean, like, specifically?"

"She was right there with me," Drake said. "She

said her head hurt. Then she asked me if it was snowing. I thought she was kidding, because it's, like, two hundred degrees out here. But then she said 'Oh,' like that. 'Oh.' The next thing I knew, she'd quit digging, and she was calling to the girls, the little girls. She seemed odd, you know. Nervous. Like she had something she had to do fast. And then I saw her with her bag, saw her taking out those bracelets, and she was leaning down close and handing them around; and then her feet were going out from under her, and one of the little girls cried, and I don't know, Georgia, I don't really know. I was just there. Just lucky enough to catch her."

"I saw it," Sophie repeated, and it seemed that that was all she knew of the story, that it was the only piece of the puzzle she had, as if she hadn't been watching, as if she had never really noticed just how too-thin Riley really was.

"It just happened," Drake said. "There wasn't time to think about it."

There wasn't time, Drake said, and all I could think of was how I'd been the one to drag Riley into this, back in the winter, when I had done my best to ignore this disease she'd been trying to hide, when Anapra was nothing more than a name to us, a place on a map, a way to get away and see the world and grow up, some more, together. I'd come to Anapra to gain perspective, to fight my battles, to let the blackbird that was my heart go free. But I'd gone missing when Riley needed me, and now here we were, headed for a clinic in a squatters' town where storms could blow down the houses and water was delivered in trucks. Way beyond, in the distance, rose the Cristo del Rey, a big white limestone cross on a hill. I prayed in its direction. I made promises I swore to God I'd keep:

No more hiding from the problems that confront me.

No more seeing mostly black in a world of so much white. "We must risk delight."

We had to travel several long blocks. We passed a house whose roof was the sawn-off roof of an old pickup truck. We crossed over power lines and the streaming sewage. In one backyard three perfectly white horses stood. I thought they were statues until one flicked its tail. Sophie saw it too, and we shivered. There was a cat fast asleep in the two-thirds part of a broken pail.

"We almost there?" Sophie leaned forward and

asked Mack, and Roberto answered, *"Sí."* Riley hadn't opened her eyes. Her skin was dry despite the heat. I saw Drake glance back at her, then search through the windows for some kind of clinic sign; and oh, how I wanted to reach out and kiss him, thank him for being there for Riley, for saving her from a concrete ditch, for me.

The clinic was beige and small. Drake carried Riley from the van just as he had carried her in; and this time when he lifted her, she moaned.

"Hey, Ri," I whispered, "it's us," holding her hand as Drake carried her forward and Mack and Roberto hurried ahead.

They spent a lot of time talking to a nurse at a desk. I spent the time talking to Riley—telling her where we were and what we were doing and how she was going to get better soon, even though I couldn't tell if she heard me. Drake just stood there with her, didn't budge, strong as the Cristo del Rey. There were children and women sprawled all over the room, waiting for doctors and cures.

"They're going to put her in a room," Sophie said,

because she'd been going back and forth between the front desk and us, trying to keep track of the plans. Now Mack started walking and Drake followed behind, and we all wove between the people who sat crowded in that hall—stepped over feet and legs and sacks and babies sitting on the floor. A nurse was just finishing putting a fresh sheet on a thin cot. Drake leaned and laid Riley down. I straightened her hair and Sophie held her hand, and now Roberto did the talking as the nurse wrote down things on a chart.

"They're cousins," Mack said to the three of us, meaning Roberto and the nurse. "Riley's in very good hands."

"They're going to start an IV," Drake said. He'd been following the conversation.

"That's good," I said. "Right?"

"Yeah," he said. "She should be fine."

She didn't look fine, though. I could see through her skin to her bones like I had the night before, and I knew that no matter what they could fix in Anapra, they'd have to fix a whole lot more at home. Riley had stopped eating to prove something to her mom, to make herself so unordinary thin; but what she'd done had hurt herself and had not in any way made her lovely.

Roberto's cousin went out and came back in, dragging one of those IV poles behind her. She made us go out into the hall while she tapped at Riley's veins. The hall was as crowded as it was before, and now there were kids poking their faces past our legs to get a look at what was going on. Little kids, pretty as the kids up the hill. All big brown eyes and colored cottons, though you could read the sickness in them, the hurt, the fact that here, too, fixing was needed.

"Georgia," Mack said, motioning to me to step away from the others and follow him down the hall. I knew what was coming. I deserved it. "You know I'm disappointed," he started. "We stay together at GoodWorks. We don't go wandering off." I waited for his anger. For repercussions; there would be some.

"I'm sorry," I said. I felt a child's sticky hands on the backs of my legs. Mack said something to the child in Spanish. I turned and saw him smiling as if he'd just won some game.

"I know you had your heart in the right place; but if you really felt you had to take Isabela home, you should have asked me first and found a partner."

"I know."

"In every good place there are bad people. Anapra's no different."

"I know that, Mack."

"I don't care if we're working in New York City. When you're with GoodWorks, you go with a partner."

I didn't answer. He'd said it enough times now. I understood.

"Riley's here in this clinic because she hasn't stayed hydrated. And frankly, Georgia, because she hasn't eaten. You understand, I'm sure, what I mean."

I nodded.

"We make our rules at GoodWorks for a reason."

"I understand. It won't happen again."

"I told your parents you'd be safe with me. But every one of you is responsible for helping me to keep that promise."

"I will."

The little boy was back at me again. I looked down and saw that he'd thrown his head straight back, trying to get my attention.

"They're going to keep Riley here this afternoon," Mack said. "I'm asking you and Sophie to stick together, stay with her. They're good people at the clinic. They are Roberto's friends; they know what they're doing. They can help Riley for right now, for today. We can help her going forward. But when she gets home, she's going to need much more than that."

"I know," I said.

"Riley has a problem."

"I know."

"No afternoon at a clinic is going to fix that."

"Yes."

"I'm taking Drake and Roberto up to the site. I'll be back for the three of you later."

I nodded, wanting to thank him. But when he smiled, his face broke up into its many sun-scribbled pieces, and for some reason that made me even sadder. Mack was old and young at the same time. Maybe the constant taking care had left him somehow lonely.

thirteen

Roberto's cousin had brought two bamboo chairs into the room and had placed them on either side of Riley's cot. She'd hung the IV bag from a metal prong above Riley's head, and a strip of thick white tape went across the place where the needle had gone under Riley's skin. The nurse had taken a second sheet and bunched it up into a pillow. Already Riley seemed less pale, the color coming back into her freckles, her thirteen earrings looking a little more like music.

"She's pretty," Sophie said; and I said, "Except she doesn't know it. I hate when that happens."

"Yeah. Me, too."

We sat there in silence, one of Riley's hands in each of ours.

"How long," Sophie asked, finally, "have you two been friends?"

"Oh my God," I said, sighing like Mariselle, leaning into my chair but keeping my hand in Riley's. And then: "Forever, I guess. Yeah. Forever." My thoughts went back to the beginning of time, and now I started telling Sophie how it was that Riley and I had met in kindergarten. It was back before Riley's dad had done his gonzo merger deal, I said, before Riley's mom had started Botox. We had been more the same than different at first. It was the sameness part of us that we grew up holding on to. "We were the queens of finger paints," I said. "We made pancakes out of mud. We got carpooled together after a while because we were that inseparable; and after school she'd come to my house, or sometimes I'd go to hers."

"You mean you've known each other for, like, a decade?" Sophie asked, incredulous, doing some math in her head, it looked like, looking from Riley's face to mine.

"Uh-huh."

"Totally," she said. "I'd give anything for a long-time friend like that. I mean, I don't know. My parents keep moving. My dad, you know: his job. I've already been to seven schools. I didn't get a shot at best friend forever. Class clown, yeah. I got that. But never best-friend-forever status."

"I'm lucky, I guess," I said.

"Guess so."

"I don't know. It's just how the cards fell."

Sophie sat as she was, leaning back against her chair; and I kept remembering, letting the pictures crop up in my head, little snapshot portraits of a friendship. "We had a tadpole farm when we were seven," I said after some time had passed. "Like, that was our big thing for a while—the tadpole farm."

"A tadpole farm?" Sophie looked at me like I was crazy.

"Yeah. I swear. We did."

"And how does *that* work?" she wanted to know.

"I'm not really sure," I said. I was trying to remember. "It was in the stream behind my house," I started. "We'd take these rocks from the banks and build up these walls in the shallowest parts of the water. Then we'd flutter the water with our hands, you know, like this"—I showed her—"to get the tadpoles in. They always scattered away, at least from what I can remember. Sometimes they came back. But for a little while they were like our own tadpoles. Like, we had names for them and everything. And then one day we went and they weren't tadpoles. They had arms and feet. They were frogs."

"I wouldn't have taken Riley for a farmer," Sophie said.

"Riley just goes with things," I said. "Always has. She's almost always good for my wacko ideas."

"Yeah?"

"Like at Halloween"—I kept going, couldn't stop myself now—"we always dressed like twins, even after I'd gotten big and she'd stayed small, and my hair got dark and hers did not, and her dad got rich and my dad's job was the same old, same old. We called ourselves the Identicals. It always made Riley laugh really hard. She'd fashion our costumes. Do the makeup. Riley's really good at costumes, hair, and makeup. At making things. Riley's great at that."

Sophie had let her hair out of its ponytail while I

was talking. It hung in thick, wild pieces around her face. She had a crease in her brow, where I suppose she kept her thoughts. She would have made someone a really good best friend.

Now looking at Riley lying there on the cot, I knew how strange my story must have seemed, how clear it had to be that Riley could have chosen anyone at all for a best friend. A girl like me doesn't have options the way girls like Riley do. A girl like me doesn't often get chosen. But Riley had stayed true, and now I'd blown it, and I felt myself getting hot with tears. "It's weird," I said. "I know. You wouldn't think it just to see us. She being so petite. Me like the Jolly Green Giant."

"The heart is not a size," Sophie said after looking between Riley's face and mine and saying nothing for a real long time.

"Oh, God," I said. A fat tear in the back of one eye got loose and started to roll and roll.

"Georgia," Sophie said, "now is, like, the exact wrong time for sad."

I looked at her to see what she meant. She gestured her chin in the direction of Riley's face.

"Hey," I said, for the sapphire eyes were open. "You

scared the hell out of us. You know that?"

"What just happened?" she asked. Her voice was soft, wisping, true. It was unguarded.

"The heat," Sophie said. "The hole."

"Exhaustion," I said. "A long time coming." I didn't say anything about anorexia or disproving average, because I knew I didn't have to. Riley bit her pale lower lip with her row of perfect upper teeth. She looked past Sophie and past me and let one tear fall from one eye. She shook her head, then touched one hand to the tape that held the IV line to the needle that fed her for now.

"I messed up," Riley said.

"You can fix it," I told her.

But she looked at me as if she wasn't precisely sure. As if the only thing she knew right then was that there were two of us, one on either side, holding her skinny hands.

"You guys," she said, and then she couldn't say more, for her shoulders were quaking, her breathing was all fits and starts. A tremble. A shiver. A sigh.

"You guys," Riley said again.

"We can fix it," I said. "I promise."

fourteen

A cloud had floated in and opened; at last the rain had come. We rode in the vans looking out at Juárez—at the gully of the river, at the dust pooling to mud, at the saturating border town where we had come, each of us bearing our secrets. Riley had her head on my shoulder and her hand in Sophie's, and nobody was talking—there wasn't any need. I caught Drake's eyes in the window. They looked straight back and into me.

By the time we reached the complex, the cloud had emptied. Beads of rain sat on the upturned faces of things and clung like glitter to the stucco walls and dazzled the thick-paned windows. At Manuel's, Leonor and Concha were busy. Above us the skies were scrubbed clean.

fifteen

At dusk we pulled the tables side by side and ate as one—Catherine, then her mom, then Jazzy, then Corey, Mariselle, Neil, and Jon on the one side; Sam, Sophie, Riley, Drake, and me on the other. At one end of the table was Mr. Thom. At the other sat Mack, lean and crinkled and talking, not teaching, as if he had joined us, somehow, crossed a bridge. We wouldn't let Riley fall again. We understood that; so did she. We understood, too, that it would not matter, not at all, where we would go with our lives after Anapra—to what internships, what colleges, what promises or problems. We'd come together there, and that would always be our fact. And that night, as the sun went low on the hills beyond, I remembered Mack, down in the basement in that Main Line space, talking about seeds. I thought of how responsibility is not just a weight but also those things that you're given the privileged chance to see. To snap into your camera for later, when you're home, when time is still the future.

After dinner was over and we'd cleared our plates, Mack suggested that we move the tables and the benches to the chapel side of the courtyard. "On the count of three," Mr. Thom said; and we all lifted, carried, set the splintery things down. Manuel was already headed up the steps when we returned—a donkey piñata hanging from one hand.

"It's been years," Mrs. K. said, shaking her head, "since I have seen one of those."

"Is that for us?" Jazzy was saying. "Really?"

You could tell that the piñata had been made by hand. It was gray with pink eyes and Irish green hooves, and the sombrero was jaunty on its floppy-eared head. Corey hammered at the air with some invisible bat, and now Manuel was rambling up the stairs. He laced a long rope through the railing and left the donkey swing-tilting from a frayed rope end. When the whole thing was rigged, Manuel came back down the steps, went into a storage room, and returned with a blunt stick.

Corey was first in line, because Corey was Corey. Everyone else lined up after him, Mrs. K. and Mr. Thom included. I was at the back of the line, between Riley and Sam. When I turned to look for Drake, I saw that he had vanished across the courtyard and was headed for the gate, where Socorro was standing.

She wore a green dress with a yellow cotton sash that was fixed in the back with a bow. On her right arm, where the goose had snapped its beak, was a sleeve of gauze. Drake had on his torn jeans, a black T-shirt, and gray flip-flops, and he held keys in one hand. Now he was leaning down and working the lock, opening the gate, inviting Socorro in. Soon she was hoisted high in Drake's arms, riding toward us on his strength, the shyest smile on her face. Soon Sophie was reaching and straightening the hem of Socorro's green skirt, and now Riley, pale Riley, was slipping every one of her twenty-two bracelets from her too-skinny wrist and gliding them up the pole of Socorro's left arm. The heart is not a size, Sophie had said; and I knew she was right—that there was no measure for the people we were becoming, no limit to what we might become.

By now the sky was the color of the purple gladiolus that grow high in my mother's garden. There were the men on the nearby roof in their spectator chairs, and there was Lobo lying low beside the chapel. Leonor and Concha had come out to watch, and Manuel stood beside them, his back against the kitchen wall. It was Mack, in the end, who took the piñata rope in hand and went up to the third plank step and began to make the donkey dance. Corey stepped up and clobbered the poor beast's hind foot. Neil got a whack at the tail. Then Mariselle gave the thing a dazzling crack; but the only thing that the donkey shed was some of its tissue-paper coat—fizzing pieces, like confetti. Next, Catherine, Jon, and Mrs. K. took their turns, but Mack was hiking the thing up and down so fast that no one had made meaningful contact.

When it was Drake's at bat, he turned to me. "Georgia," he asked, "do you mind?" He leaned down so that I could reach Socorro—take her into my arms and keep her safe. We all stepped back then as Drake assumed a slugger's stance eyeing the dangling donkey that Mack was swinging all around. The donkey went up and down—smashed up but still holding, shedding but not letting anyone close to its candy—but Drake never lost his focus, didn't give in, even as we hollered, "Take it down, Drake. Show it your business, Drake. Show it what you're made of." We were calling, and the men on the roof were calling, and Leonor and Concha were laughing, and in my arms Socorro was perfectly still, a look of wonder on her face.

But Drake did nothing until Drake was ready. He let the poor beast dangle and Mack work the rope, and then he turned and fixed his eyes on me. "This one's for Georgia," he said; and the next time that donkey entered smack into Drake's strike zone, he let go with a magnificent whack. It was a beautiful, single, super-clean swing. It sliced the donkey from neck to tail. But still the donkey hung above us and not a piece of candy fell.

Riley curtsied as Drake now handed her the stick. He bowed and said, "All yours." The stick was bigger by far than both of Riley's arms together, but she took it in both hands and lifted it high above her head. We started chanting her name, as if it were the bottom of the ninth, all bases loaded and two outs. Drake was standing close beside me now, and I was leaning toward him, slipping within his shadow.

On the third plank of the step, Mack kept making that donkey dance, pulling the rope up and down, being careful with it now so that it wouldn't split in two before Riley got her chance. "Ri-LEY. Ri-LEY. Ri-LEY," we were chanting, and the rooftop men were chanting, and Lobo was running in wolf circles barking, and the thirteen earrings in Riley's ear sparkled. She was wearing a pale yellow skirt and a neat white tank and a Band-Aid over the place where the IV line had gone in. The high part of the stick was trembling above her head; and Mack had this smile on his face as he pulled the donkey tricks, a smile that I'm sure I'm never forgetting. Riley bent her knees and flexed her elbows, her wrists. She focused her eyes, pursed her lips. When Mack let the donkey down into her zone, she stepped back and into one long, gorgeous, perfect swing—nothing anyone would ever count as average. The candies spun out high and far, over the roof, past the gates. It was as if she'd set a million stars free to shimmer in whatever ways they wished.

The moon was a perfect half, and I couldn't remember if it was waxing or waning, another of Buzzby's favorite paired words. I could only see how everything was happening at once—the sun still setting and the moon still rising, and Drake leaning toward me close.

That's when I felt Socorro stretch skyward with her arms—reach for a figment I couldn't see, then struggle to reach farther. It was as if I were holding a pair of wings in my arms, a beating something.

"Esmeralda," Socorro said. "Esmeralda," her voice a pure, sweet sound above the courtyard's happy chaos, her tiny body so alive and urgent, so extremely true and present.

I turned and saw that Drake was watching me, his complicated goodness right there on the surface, within reach. "Her sister," he told me, and Socorro said the name again—Esmeralda—then reached for Drake so as to be lifted higher. I felt the weight of her vanish into Drake's arms; I saw her arms go up, toward the sky. I heard her cry out again, and that's when I saw what she was seeing: a pure white cloud belted by a band of gold, a horizontal offering.

Happiness floats, I thought. It is the color of a truce. I closed my eyes and opened them, and it wasn't just the ghost of Socorro's sister up there; it was my own anxious heart set free.

"Hey, Georgia." I heard Riley now from across the courtyard, where she was still collecting the spoils of her work with Sophie, Mariselle, and the others. "What'd you think?" She flexed her skinny arm and popped a sour ball into her mouth.

"Most outstanding, Riley," I said, and she laughed; and that, in that ruthless furnace, was the everlasting thing. Because no one ever laughed like Ri.

Acknowledgments

The Heart Is Not a Size began as so much of my work does—not as a novel, but as a series of impressions glimpsed, gained, lost, and finally resurrected.

In this case, it began with a trip I was privileged to take with the adults and youth of St. John's Presbyterian Church. Like the characters in this story, we traveled from the Main Line near Philadelphia to the squatters' village called Anapra. We drove the streets, slept beneath a cross, went out on the bleached, white roads, and always were graced by the exceptional beauty and generosity of the local families who embraced our efforts to build a community bathroom. My Salvadoran husband, Bill, came along as interpreter and architect. My son, Jeremy, loaded sand and hammered frames and yielded his impeccable perspective. Victor Wilson, Dave Exley, Karen Black, Brian Bouvier, Libby Dalyrmple, Tom Higgins, Janette Scott, Kathy Shaw, John Shaw, and Karen Sheep paved the way with intelligence, fortitude, blinding good humor, and ponderable but never ponderous stories. Joe Apathy, Katie Babiy, Kelly Birmingham, Kyle Birmingham, Meredith

Bouvier, Michael Browne, Sammy Browne, Josh Chudy, Sarah Ciarrochi, Christine Cummins, Charlie Dalrymple, Elizabeth Dalrymple, Taylor Eschbach, Dustin Gilmour, Maureen Higgins, Billy Hudson, Matt Kaminskas, Alex Klebe, Mark Moeller, Danny Scott, Kaitlyn Shaw, and Nina Shaw made the trip profoundly unforgettable and left me feeling so infinitely lucky to have spent the days with them. They have gone on to exceptional things, these exquisite young people; the world has opened to them.

I took a camera to Juárez and published two photo-essays in the *Pennsylvania Gazette* and *Haverford*; thank you to editors John Prendergast and Chris Mills, respectively. I had an idea for a novel—a vaguely articulated one—and Laura Geringer was kind enough to place her faith in the inchoative. Jill Santopolo brought her insight, humor, intelligence, and commitment to the final drafts; she brought her cherished friendship. Carla Weise stayed the cover design course, as she always brilliantly does. Ruta Rimas, always the glue on the Harper team, stepped in as my editor as the book began to make its way into the world; she has enthusiasm and she has passion—just what this writer needs. Renée

Cafiero made this a better book; she always does. Laura Kaplan sent out word. My thanks to Amy Rennert, who picks up the phone when I call and tells me the truth; we need truth tellers as our friends and agents.

To the people of Juárez, who have in the years since I journeyed there been faced with horrific, rising violence and terrifying challenges, I express my great thanks for their hospitality and my deepest hope for healing.

I am grateful, finally, to Kenneth Kane, a rising, bighearted writer with whom I shared treasured conversations about words, books, and the great poet Jack Gilbert.